The Grim Smile of the Five Towns

by

Arnold Bennett

The Echo Library 2005

Published by

The Echo Library

Paperbackshop Ltd
Cockrup Farm House
Coln St Aldwyns
Cirencester GL7 5AZ

www.echo-library.com

ISBN 1-84637-662-9

THE GRIM SMILE OF THE FIVE TOWNS

ARNOLD BENNETT

To my old and constant friend
JOSEPH DAWSON
a student profoundly versed
in the human nature of
the Five Towns

CONTENTS

THE LION'S SHARE

I

In the Five Towns the following history is related by those who know it as something side-splittingly funny—as one of the best jokes that ever occurred in a district devoted to jokes. And I, too, have hitherto regarded it as such. But upon my soul, now that I come to write it down, it strikes me as being, after all, a pretty grim tragedy. However, you shall judge, and laugh or cry as you please.

It began in the little house of Mrs Carpole, up at Bleakridge, on the hill between Bursley and Hanbridge. Mrs Carpole was the second Mrs Carpole, and her husband was dead. She had a stepson, Horace, and a son of her own, Sidney. Horace is the hero, or the villain, of the history. On the day when the unfortunate affair began he was nineteen years old, and a model youth. Not only was he getting on in business, not only did he give half his evenings to the study of the chemistry of pottery and the other half to various secretaryships in connection with the Wesleyan Methodist Chapel and Sunday-school, not only did he save money, not only was he a comfort to his stepmother and a sort of uncle to Sidney, not only was he an early riser, a total abstainer, a non-smoker, and a good listener; but, in addition to the practice of these manifold and rare virtues, he found time, even at that tender age, to pay his tailor's bill promptly and to fold his trousers in the same crease every night—so that he always looked neat and dignified. Strange to say, he made no friends. Perhaps he was just a thought too perfect for a district like the Five Towns; a sin or so might have endeared him to the entire neighbourhood. Perhaps his loneliness was due to his imperfect sense of humour, or perhaps to the dull, unsmiling heaviness of his somewhat flat features.

Sidney was quite a different story. Sidney, to use his mother's phrase, was a little jockey. His years were then eight. Fair- haired and blue-eyed, as most little jockeys are, he had a smile and a scowl that were equally effective in tyrannizing over both his mother and Horace, and he was beloved by everybody. Women turned to look at him in the street. Unhappily, his health was not good. He was afflicted by a slight deafness, which, however, the doctor said he would grow out of; the doctor predicted for him a lusty manhood. In the meantime, he caught every disease that happened to be about, and nearly died of each one. His latest acquisition had been scarlet fever. Now one afternoon, after he had 'peeled' and his room had been disinfected, and he was beginning to walk again, Horace came home and decided that Sidney should be brought downstairs for tea as a treat, to celebrate his convalescence, and that he, Horace, would carry him downstairs. Mrs Carpole was delighted with the idea, and Sidney also, except that Sidney did not want to be carried downstairs—he wanted to walk down.

'I think it will be better for him to walk, Horace dear,' said Mrs Carpole, in her thin, plaintive voice. 'He can, quite well. And you know how clumsy you are. Supposing you were to fall!'

Horace, nevertheless, in pursuance of his programme of being uncle to Sidney, was determined to carry Sidney. And carry Sidney he did, despite warnings and kickings. At least he carried him as far as the turn in the steep stairs, at which point he fell, just as his stepmother had feared, and Sidney with him. The half-brothers arrived on the ground floor in company, but Horace, with his eleven stone two, was on top, and the poor suffering little convalescent lay moveless and insensible.

It took the doctor forty minutes to bring him to, and all the time the odour of grilled herrings, which formed part of the uneaten tea, made itself felt through the house like a Satanic comment on the spectacle of human life. The scene was dreadful at first. The agony then passed. There were no bruises on the boy, not a mark, and in a couple of hours he seemed to be perfectly himself. Horace breathed again, and thanked Heaven it was no worse. His gratitude to Heaven was, however, slightly premature, for in the black middle of the night poor Sidney was seized with excruciating pains in the head, and the doctor lost four hours' sleep. These pains returned at intervals of a few days, and naturally the child's convalescence was retarded. Then Horace said that Airs Carpole should take Sidney to Buxton for a fortnight, and he paid all the expenses of the trip out of his savings. He was desolated, utterly stricken; he said he should never forgive himself. Sidney improved, slowly.

II

After several months, during which Horace had given up all his limited spare time to the superintendence of the child's first steps in knowledge, Sidney was judged to be sufficiently strong to go to school, and it was arranged that he should attend the Endowed School at the Wedgwood Institution. Horace accompanied him thither on the opening day of the term—it was an inclement morning in January—and left the young delicate sprig, apparently joyous and content, to the care of his masters and the mercy of his companions. But Sidney came home for dinner weeping—weeping in spite of his new mortar-board cap, his new satchel, his new box of compasses, and his new books. His mother kept him at home in the afternoon, and by the evening another of those terrible attacks had supervened. The doctor and Horace and Mrs Carpole once more lost much precious sleep. The mysterious malady continued. School was out of the question.

And when Sidney took the air, in charge of his mother, everybody stopped to sympathize with him and to stroke his curls and call him a poor dear, and also to commiserate Mrs Carpole. As for Horace, Bursley tried to feel sorry for Horace, but it only succeeded in showing Horace that it was hiding a sentiment of indignation against him. Each friendly face as it passed Horace in the street said, without words, 'There goes the youth who probably ruined his young stepbrother's life. And through sheer obstinacy too! He dropped the little darling in spite of warnings and protests, and then fell on the top of him. Of course, he didn't do it on purpose, but—'

The doctor mentioned Greatorex of Manchester, the celebrated brain specialist. And Horace took Sidney to Manchester. They had to wait an hour and a quarter to see Greatorex, his well-known consulting- rooms in John Dalton Street being crowded with imperfect brains; but their turn came at last, and they found themselves in Greatorex's presence. Greatorex was a fat man, with the voice of a thin man, who seemed to spend the whole of his career in the care of his fingernails.

'Well, my little fellow,' said Greatorex, 'don't cry.' (For Sidney was already crying.) And then to Horace, in a curt tone: 'What is it?'

And Horace was obliged to humiliate himself and relate the accident in detail, together with all that had subsequently happened.

'Yes, yes, yes, yes!' Greatorex would punctuate the recital, and when tired of 'yes' he would say 'Hum, hum, hum, hum!'

When he had said 'hum' seventy-two times he suddenly remarked that his fee was three guineas, and told Horace to strengthen Sidney all he could, not to work him too hard, and to bring him back in a year's time.

Horace paid the money, Greatorex emitted a final 'hum', and then the stepbrothers were whisked out by an expeditious footman. The experience cost Horace over four pounds and the loss of a day's time. And the worst was that Sidney had a violent attack that very night.

School being impossible for him, Sidney had intermittent instruction from professors of both sexes at home. But he learnt practically nothing except the banjo. Horace had to buy him a banjo: it cost the best part of a ten-pound note; still, Horace could do no less. Sidney's stature grew rapidly; his general health certainly improved, yet not completely; he always had a fragile, interesting air. Moreover, his deafness did not disappear: there were occasions when it was extremely pronounced. And he was never quite safe from these attacks in the head. He spent a month or six weeks each year in the expensive bracing atmosphere of some seaside resort, and altogether he was decidedly a heavy drain on Horace's resources. People were aware of this, and they said that Horace ought to be happy that he was in a position to spend money freely on his poor brother. Had not the doctor predicted, before the catastrophe due to Horace's culpable negligence, that Sidney would grow into a strong man, and that his deafness would leave him? The truth was, one never knew the end of those accidents in infancy! Further, was not Sidney's sad condition slowly killing his mother? It was whispered about that, since the disaster, Sidney had not been QUITE sound mentally. Was not the mere suspicion of this enough to kill any mother?

And, as a fact, Mrs Carpole did die. She died of quinsy, doubtless aggravated by Sidney's sad condition.

Not long afterwards Horace came into a small fortune from his maternal grandfather. But poor Sidney did not come into any fortune, and people somehow illogically inferred that Horace had not behaved quite nicely in coming into a fortune while his suffering invalid brother, whom he had so deeply harmed, came into nothing. Even Horace had compunctions due to the visitations of a similar idea. And with part of the fortune he bought a house with a large garden up at Toft End, the highest hill of the hilly Five Towns, so that Sidney might have the benefit of the air. He also engaged a housekeeper and servants. With the remainder of the fortune he obtained a partnership in the firm of earthenware manufacturers for whom he had been acting as highly-paid manager.

Sidney reached the age of eighteen, and was most effective to look upon, his bright hair being still curly, and his eyes a wondrous blue, and his form elegant; and the question of Sidney's future arose. His health was steadily on the up grade. The deafness had quite disappeared. He had inclinations towards art, and had already amused himself by painting some beautiful vases. So it was settled that he should enter Horace's works on the art side, with a view to becoming, ultimately, art director. Horace gave him three pounds a week, in order that he might feel perfectly independent, and, to the same end, Sidney paid Horace seven-and-sixpence a week for board and lodging. But the change of life upset the youth's health again. After only two visits to the works he had a grave recurrence of the head-attacks, and he was solemnly exhorted not to apply himself too closely to business. He therefore took several half-holidays a week, and sometimes a whole one. And even when he put in one of his full days he would arrive at the works three hours after Horace, and restore the balance by leaving an hour earlier. The entire town watched over him as a mother watches over a son. The notion that he was not QUITE right in the pate gradually died away, and everybody was thankful for that, though it was feared an untimely grave might be his portion.

III

She was a nice girl: the nicest girl that Horace had ever met with, because her charming niceness included a faculty of being really serious about serious things—and yet she could be deliciously gay. In short, she was a revelation to Horace. And her name was Ella, and she had come one year to spend some weeks with Mrs Penkethman, the widowed headmistress of the Wesleyan Day School, who was her cousin. Mrs Penkethman and Ella had been holidaying together in France; their arrival in Bursley naturally coincided with the reopening of the school in August for the autumn term.

Now at this period Horace was rather lonely in his large house and garden; for Sidney, in pursuit of health, had gone off on a six weeks' cruise round Holland, Finland, Norway, and Sweden, in one of those Atlantic liners which, translated like Enoch without dying, become in their old age 'steam-yachts', with fine names apt to lead to confusion with the private yacht of the Tsar of Russia. Horace had offered him the trip, and Horace was also paying his weekly salary as usual.

So Horace, who had always been friendly with Mrs Penkethman, grew now more than ever friendly with Mrs Penkethman. And Mrs Penkethman and Ella were inseparable. The few aristocrats left in Bursley in September remarked that Horace knew what he was about, as it was notorious that Ella had the most solid expectations. But as a matter of fact Horace did not know what he was about, and he never once thought of Ella's expectations. He was simply, as they say in Bursley, knocked silly by Ella. He honestly imagined her to be the wonderfullest woman on the earth's surface, with her dark eyes and her expressive sympathetic gestures, and her alterations of seriousness and gaiety. It astounded him that a girl of twenty- one could have thought so deeply upon life as she had. The inexplicable thing was that she looked up to HIM. She evidently admired HIM. He wanted to tell her that she was quite wrong about him, much too kind in her estimate of him—that really he was a very ordinary man indeed. But another instinct prevented him from thus undeceiving her.

And one Saturday afternoon, the season being late September, Horace actually got those two women up to tea in his house and garden. He had not dared to dream of such bliss. He had hesitated long before asking them to come, and in asking them he had blushed and stammered: the invitation had seemed to him to savour of audacity. But, bless you! they had accepted with apparent ecstasy. They gave him to think that they had genuinely wanted to come. And they came extra-specially dressed—visions, lilies of the field. And as the day was quite warm, tea was served in the garden, and everybody admired the view; and there was no restraint, no awkwardness. In particular Ella talked with an ease and a distinction that enchanted Horace, and almost made him talk with ease and distinction too. He said to himself that, seeing he had only known her a month, he was getting on amazingly. He said to himself that his good luck passed belief.

Then there was a sound of cab-wheels on the other side of the garden-wall, and presently Horace heard the housekeeper complimenting Sidney on his good looks, and Sidney asking the housekeeper to lend him three shillings to pay the cabman. The golden youth had returned without the slightest warning from his cruise. The tea trio, at the lower end of the garden, saw him standing in the porch, tanned, curly, graceful, and young. Horace half rose, and then sat down again. Ella stared hard.

'That must be your brother,' she said.

'Yes, that's Sid,' Horace answered; and then, calling out loudly: 'Come down here, Sid, and tell them to bring another cup and saucer.'

'Right you are, old man,' Sidney shouted. 'You see I'm back. What! Mrs Penkethman, is that you?' He came down the central path of the garden like a Narcissus.

'He DOES look delicate,' said Ella under her breath to Horace. Tears came to her eyes.

Naturally Ella knew all about Sidney. She enjoyed the entire confidence of Mrs Penkethman, and what Mrs Penkethman didn't know of the private history of the upper classes in Bursley did not amount to very much.

These were nearly the last words that Ella spoke to Horace that afternoon. The introduction was made, and Sidney slipped into the party as comfortably as he slipped into everything, like a candle slipping into a socket. But nevertheless Ella talked no more. She just stared at Sidney, and listened to him. Horace was proud that Sidney had made such an impression on her; he was glad that she showed no aversion to Sidney, because, in the event of Horace's marriage, where would Sidney live, if not with Horace and Horace's wife? Still, he could have wished that Ella would continue to display her conversational powers.

Presently, Sidney lighted a cigarette. He was of those young men whose delicate mouths seem to have been fashioned for the nice conduct of a cigarette. And he had a way of blowing out the smoke that secretly ravished every feminine beholder. Horace still held to his boyhood's principles; but he envied Sidney a little.

At the conclusion of the festivity these two women naturally could not be permitted to walk home alone. And, naturally, also, the four could not walk abreast on the narrow pavements. Horace went first with Mrs Penkethman. He was mad with anxiety to appropriate Ella, but he dared not. It would not have been quite correct; it would have been, as they say in Bursley, too thick. Besides, there was the question of age. Horace was over thirty, and Mrs Penkethman was also—over thirty; whereas Sidney was twenty-one, and so was Ella. Hence Sidney walked behind with Ella, and the procession started in silence. Horace did not look round too often—that would not have been quite proper—but whenever he did look round the other couple had lagged farther and farther behind, and Ella seemed perfectly to have recovered her speech. At length he looked round, and lo! they had not turned the last corner; and they arrived at Mrs Penkethman's cottage at Hillport a quarter of an hour after their elders.

IV

The wedding cost Horace a large sum of money. You see, he could not do less than behave handsomely by the bride, owing to his notorious admiration for her; and of course the bridegroom needed setting up. Horace practically furnished their home for them out of his own pocket; it was not to be expected that Sidney should have resources. Further, Sidney as a single man, paying seven-and- six a week for board and lodging, could no doubt struggle along upon three pounds weekly. But Sidney as a husband, with the nicest girl in the world to take care of, and house-rent to pay, could not possibly perform the same feat. Although he did no more work at the manufactory—Horace could not have been so unbrotherly as to demand it—Horace paid him eight pounds a week instead of three.

And the affair cost Horace a good deal besides money. But what could Horace do? He decidedly would not have wished to wreck the happiness of two young and beautiful lives, even had he possessed the power to do so. And he did not possess the power. Those two did not consult Horace before falling in love. They merely fell in love, and there was an end of it—and an end of Horace too! Horace had to suffer. He did suffer.

Perhaps it was for his highest welfare that other matters came to monopolize his mind. One sorrow drives out another. If you sit on a pin you are apt to forget that you have the toothache. The earthenware manufactory was not going well. Plenty of business was being done, but not at the right prices. Crushed between the upper and nether millstones of the McKinley Tariff and German competition, Horace, in company with other manufacturers, was breathing out his life's blood in the shape of capital. The truth was that he had never had enough capital. He had heavily mortgaged the house at Toft End in order to purchase his partners' shares in the business and have the whole undertaking to himself, and he profoundly regretted it. He needed every penny that he could collect; the strictest economy was necessary if he meant to survive the struggle. And here he was paying eight pounds a week to a personage purely ornamental, after having squandered hundreds in rendering that personage comfortable! The situation was dreadful.

You may ask, Why did he not explain the situation to Sidney? Well, partly because he was too kind, and partly because he was too proud, and partly because Sidney would not have understood. Horace fought on, keeping up a position in the town and hoping that miracles would occur.

Then Ella's expectations were realized. Sidney and she had some twenty thousand pounds to play with. And they played the most agreeable games. But not in Bursley. No. They left Horace in Bursley and went to Llandudno for a spell. Horace envied them, but he saw them off at the station as an elder brother should, and tipped the porters.

Certainly he was relieved of the formality of paying eight pounds a week to his brother. But this did not help him much. The sad fact was that 'things' (by which is meant fate, circumstances, credit, and so on) had gone too far. It was no longer a question of eight pounds a week; it was a question of final ruin.

Surely he might have borrowed money from Sidney? Sidney had no money; the money was Ella's, and Horace could not have brought himself to borrow money from a woman—from Ella, from a heavenly creature who always had a soothing sympathetic word for him. That would have been to take advantage of Ella. No, if you suggest such a thing, you do not know Horace.

I stated in the beginning that he had no faults. He was therefore absolutely honest. And he called his creditors together while he could yet pay them twenty shillings in the pound. It was a noble act, rare enough in the Five Towns and in other parts of England. But he received no praise for it. He had only done what every man in his position ought to do. If Horace had failed for ten times the sum that his debts actually did amount to, and then paid two shillings in the pound instead of twenty, he would have made a stir in the world and been looked up to as no ordinary man of business.

Having settled his affairs in this humdrum, idiotic manner, Horace took a third-class return to Llandudno. Sidney and Ella were staying at the hydro with the strange Welsh name, and he found Sidney lolling on the sunshiny beach in front of the hydro discoursing on the banjo to himself. When asked where his wife was, Sidney replied that she was lying down, and was obliged to rest as much as possible.

Horace, ashamed to trouble this domestic idyl, related his misfortunes as airily as he could.

And Sidney said he was awfully sorry, and had no notion how matters stood, and could he do anything for Horace? If so, Horace might—

'No,' said Horace. 'I'm all right. I've very fortunately got an excellent place as manager in a big new manufactory in Germany.' (This is how we deal with German competition in the Five Towns.)

'Germany?' cried Sidney.

'Yes,' said Horace; 'and I start the day after tomorrow.'

'Well,' said Sidney, 'at any rate you'll stay the night.'

'Thanks,' said Horace, 'you're very kind. I will.'

So they went into the hydro together, Sidney caressing his wonderful new pearl-inlaid banjo; and Horace talked in low tones to Ella as she lay on the sofa. He convinced Ella that his departure to Germany was the one thing he had desired all his life, because it was not good that Ella should be startled, shocked, or grieved.

They dined well.

But in the night Sidney had a recurrence of his old illness—a bad attack; and Horace sat up through the dark hours, fetched the doctor, and bought things at the chemist's. Towards morning Sidney was better. And Horace, standing near the bed, gazed at his stepbrother and tried in his stupid way to read the secrets beneath that curly hair. But he had no success. He caught himself calculating how much Sidney had cost him, at periods of his career when he could ill spare money; and, having caught himself, he was angry with himself for such baseness. At eight o'clock he ventured to knock at Ella's door and explain to her that Sidney had not been quite well. She had passed a peaceful night, for he had, of course, refrained from disturbing her.

He was not quite sure whether Sidney had meant him to stay at the hydro as his guest, so he demanded a bill, paid it, said good-bye, and left for Bonn-on-the-Rhine. He was very exhausted and sleepy. Happily the third-class carriages on the London & North-Western are pretty comfortable. Between Chester and Crewe he had quite a doze, and dreamed that he had married Ella after all, and that her twenty thousand pounds had put the earthenware business on a footing of magnificent and splendid security.

V

A few months later Horace's house and garden at Toft End were put up to auction by arrangement with his mortgagee and his trade- creditors. And Sidney was struck with the idea of buying the place. The impression was that it would go cheap. Sidney said it would be a pity to let the abode pass out of the family. Ella said that the idea of buying it was a charming one, because in the garden it was that she had first met her Sidney. So the place was duly bought, and Sidney and Ella went to live there.

Several years elapsed.

Then one day little Horace was informed that his uncle Horace, whom he had never seen, was coming to the house on a visit, and that he must be a good boy, and polite to his uncle, and all the usual sort of thing.

And in effect Horace the elder did arrive in the afternoon. He found no one to meet him at the station, or at the garden gate of the pleasaunce that had once been his, or even at the front door. A pert parlour-maid told him that her master and mistress were upstairs in the nursery, and that he was requested to go up. And he went up, and to be sure Sidney met him at the top of the stairs, banjo in hand, cigarette in mouth, smiling, easy and elegant as usual—not a trace of physical weakness in his face or form. And Horace was jocularly ushered into the nursery and introduced to his nephew. Ella had changed. She was no longer slim, and no longer gay and serious by turns. She narrowly missed being stout, and she was continuously gay, like Sidney. The child was also gay. Everybody was glad to see Horace, but nobody seemed deeply interested in Horace's affairs. As a fact he had done rather well in Germany, and had now come back to England in order to assume a working partnership in a small potting concern at Hanbridge. He was virtually beginning life afresh. But what concerned Sidney and Ella was themselves and their offspring. They talked incessantly about the infinitesimal details of their daily existence, and the alterations which they had made, or meant to make, in the house and garden. And occasionally Sidney thrummed a tune on the banjo to amuse the infant. Horace had expected them to be curious about Germany and his life in Germany. But not a bit! He might have come in from the next street and left them only yesterday, for all the curiosity they exhibited.

'Shall we go down to the drawing-room and have tea, eh?' said Ella.

'Yes, let's go and kill the fatted calf,' said Sidney.

And strangely enough, inexplicably enough, Horace did feel like a prodigal.

Sidney went off with his precious banjo, and Ella picked up sundry belongings without which she never travelled about the house.

'You carry me down-stairs, unky?' the little nephew suggested, with an appealing glance at his new uncle. 'No,' said Horace, 'I'm dashed if I do!'

BABY'S BATH

I

Mrs Blackshaw had a baby. It would be an exaggeration to say that the baby interested the entire town, Bursley being an ancient, blase sort of borough of some thirty thousand inhabitants. Babies, in fact, arrived in Bursley at the rate of more than a thousand every year. Nevertheless, a few weeks after the advent of Mrs Blackshaw's baby, when the medical officer of health reported to the Town Council that the births for the month amounted to ninety- five, and that the birth-rate of Bursley compared favourably with the birth-rates of the sister towns, Hanbridge, Knype, Longshaw, and Turnhill—when the medical officer read these memorable words at the monthly meeting of the Council, and the Staffordshire Signal reported them, and Mrs Blackshaw perused them, a blush of pride spread over Mrs Blackshaw's face, and she picked up the baby's left foot and gave it a little peck of a kiss. She could not help feeling that the real solid foundation of that formidable and magnificent output of babies was her baby. She could not help feeling that she had done something for the town—had caught the public eye.

As for the baby, except that it was decidedly superior to the average infant in external appearance and pleasantness of disposition, it was, in all essential characteristics, a typical baby—that is to say, it was purely sensuous and it lived the life of the senses. It was utterly selfish. It never thought of anyone but itself. It honestly imagined itself to be the centre of the created universe. It was convinced that the rest of the universe had been brought into existence solely for the convenience and pleasure of it—the baby. When it wanted anything it made no secret of the fact, and it was always utterly unscrupulous in trying to get what it wanted. If it could have obtained the moon it would have upset all the astronomers of Europe and made Whitaker's Almanack unsalable without a pang. It had no god but its stomach. It never bothered its head about higher things. It was a bully and a coward, and it treated women as beings of a lower order than men. In a word, it was that ideal creature, sung of the poets, from which we gradually sink and fall away as we grow older.

At the age of six months it had quite a lot of hair, and a charming rosy expanse at the back of its neck, caused through lying on its back in contemplation of its own importance. It didn't know the date of the Battle of Hastings, but it knew with the certainty of absolute knowledge that it was master of the house, and that the activity of the house revolved round it.

Now, the baby loved its bath. In any case its bath would have been an affair of immense and intricate pomp; but the fact that it loved its bath raised the interest and significance of the bath to the nth power. The bath took place at five o'clock in the evening, and it is not too much to say that the idea of the bath was immanent in the very atmosphere of the house. When you have an appointment with the dentist at five o'clock in the afternoon the idea of the appointment is immanent in your mind from the first moment of your awakening. Conceive that an appointment with the dentist implies heavenly joy instead of infernal pain, and you will have a notion of the daily state of Mrs Blackshaw and Emmie (the nurse) with regard to the baby's bath.

Even at ten in the morning Emmie would be keeping an eye on the kitchen fire, lest the cook might let it out. And shortly after noon Mrs Blackshaw would be keeping an eye on the thermometer in the bedroom where the bath occurred. From four o'clock onwards the clocks in the house were spied on and overlooked like suspected persons; but they were used to that, because the baby had his sterilized milk every two hours. I have at length allowed you to penetrate the secret of his sex.

And so at five o'clock precisely the august and exciting ceremony began in the best bedroom. A bright fire was burning (the month being December), and the carefully-shaded electric lights were also burning. A large bath-towel was spread in a convenient place on the floor, and on the towel were two chairs facing each other, and a table. On one chair was the bath, and on the other was Mrs Blackshaw with her sleeves rolled up, and on Mrs Blackshaw was another towel, and on that towel was Roger (the baby). On the table were zinc ointment, vaseline, scentless eau de Cologne, Castile soap, and a powder-puff.

Emmie having pretty nearly filled the bath with a combination of hot and cold waters, dropped the floating thermometer into it, and then added more waters until the thermometer indicated the precise temperature proper for a baby's bath. But you are not to imagine that Mrs Blackshaw trusted a mere thermometer. No. She put her arm in the water up to the elbow. She reckoned the sensitive skin near the elbow was worth forty thermometers.

Emmie was chiefly an audience. Mrs Blackshaw had engaged her as a nurse, but she could have taught a nigger-boy to do all that she allowed the nurse to do. During the bath Mrs Blackshaw and Emmie hated and scorned each other, despite their joy. Emmie was twice Mrs Blackshaw's age, besides being twice her weight, and she knew twice as much about babies as Mrs Blackshaw did. However, Mrs Blackshaw had the terrific advantage of being the mother of that particular infant, and she could always end an argument when she chose, and in her own favour. It was unjust, and Emmie felt it to be unjust; but this is not a world of justice.

Roger, though not at all precocious, was perfectly aware of the carefully-concealed hostility between his mother and his nurse, and often, with his usual unscrupulousness, he used it for his own ends. He was sitting upon his mother's knees toying with the edge of the bath, already tasting its delights in advance. Mrs Blackshaw undressed the upper half of him, and then she laid him on the flat of his back and undressed the lower half of him, but keeping some wisp of a garment round his equatorial regions. And then she washed his face with a sponge and the Castile soap, very gently, but not half gently enough for Emmie, nor half gently enough for Roger, for Roger looked upon this part of the business as insulting and superfluous. He breathed hard and kicked his feet nearly off.

'Yes, it's dreadful having our face washed, isn't it?' said Mrs Blackshaw, with her sleeves up, and her hair by this time down. 'We don't like it, do we? Yes, yes.'

Emmie grunted, without a sound, and yet Mrs Blackshaw heard her, and finished that face quickly and turned to the hands.

'Potato-gardens every day,' she said. 'Evzy day-day. Enough of that, Colonel!' (For, after all, she had plenty of spirit.) 'Fat little creases! Fat little creases! There! He likes that! There! Feet! Feet! Feet and legs! Then our back. And then WHUP we shall go into the bath! That's it. Kick! Kick your mother!'

And she turned him over.

'Incredible bungler!' said the eyes of the nurse. 'Can't she turn him over neater than that?'

'Harridan!' said the eyes of Mrs Blackshaw. 'I wouldn't let you bath him for twenty thousand pounds!'

Roger continued to breathe hard, as if his mother were a horse and he were rubbing her down.

'Now! Zoop! Whup!' cried his mother, and having deprived him of his final rag, she picked him up and sat him in the bath, and he was divinely happy, and so were the women. He appeared a gross little animal in the bath, all the tints of his flesh shimmering under the electric light. His chest was superb, but the rolled and creased bigness of his inordinate stomach was simply appalling, not to mention his great thighs and calves. The truth was, he had grown so that if he had been only a little bit bigger, he would have burst the bath. He resembled an old man who had been steadily eating too much for about forty years.

His two womenfolk now candidly and openly worshipped him, forgetting sectarian differences.

And he splashed. Oh! he splashed. You see, he had learnt how to splash, and he had certainly got an inkling that to splash was wicked and messy. So he splashed—in his mother's face, in Emmie's face, in the fire. He pretty well splashed the fire out. Ten minutes before, the bedroom had been tidy, a thing of beauty. It was now naught but a wild welter of towels, socks, binders—peninsulas of clothes nearly surrounded by water.

Finally his mother seized him again, and, rearing his little legs up out of the water, immersed the whole of his inflated torso beneath the surface.

'Hallo!' she exclaimed. 'Did the water run over his mouf? Did it?'

'Angels and ministers of grace defend us! How clumsy she is!' commented the eyes of Emmie.

'There! I fink that's about long enough for this kind of wevver,' said the mother.

'I should think it was! There's almost a crust of ice on the water now!' the nurse refrained from saying.

And Roger, full of regrets, was wrenched out of the bath. He had ceased breathing hard while in the water, but he began again immediately he emerged.

'We don't like our face wiped, do we?' said his mother on his behalf. 'We want to go back into that bath. We like it. It's more fun than anything that happens all day long! Eh? That old dandruff's coming up in fine style. It's a-peeling off like anything.'

And all the while she wiped him, patted eau de Cologne into him with the flat of her hand, and rubbed zinc ointment into him, and massaged him, and powdered him, and turned him over and over and over, till he was thoroughly well basted and cooked. And he kept on breathing hard.

Then he sneezed, amid general horror!

'I told you so!' the nurse didn't say, and she rushed to the bed where all the idol's beautiful, clean, aired things were lying safe from splashings, and handed a flannel shirt, about two inches in length, to Mrs Blackshaw. And Mrs Blackshaw rolled the left sleeve of it into a wad and stuck it over his arm, and his poor little vaccination marks were hidden from view till next morning. Roger protested.

'We don't like clothes, do we?' said his mother. 'We want to tumble back into our tub. We aren't much for clothes anyway. We'se a little Hottentot, aren't we?'

And she gradually covered him with one garment or another until there was nothing left of him but his head and his hands and feet. And she sat him up on her knees, so as to fasten his things behind. And then it might have been observed that he was no longer breathing hard, but giving vent to a sound between a laugh and a cry, while sucking his thumb and gazing round the room.

'That's our little affected cry that we start for our milk, isn't it?' his mother explained to him.

And he agreed that it was.

And before Emmie could fly across the room for the bottle, all ready and waiting, his mouth, in the shape of a perfect rectangle, had monopolized five-sixths of his face, and he was scarlet and bellowing with impatience.

He took the bottle like a tiger his prey, and seized his mother's hand that held the bottle, and he furiously pumped the milk into that insatiable gulf of a stomach. But he found time to gaze about the room too. A tear stood in each roving eye, caused by the effort of feeding.

'Yes, that's it,' said his mother. 'Now look round and see what's happening. Curiosity! Well, if you WILL bob your head, I can't help it.'

'Of course you can!' the nurse didn't say.

Then he put his finger into his mouth side by side with the bottle, and gagged himself, and choked, and gave a terrible— excuse the word—hiccough. After which he seemed to lose interest in the milk, and the pumping operations slackened and then ceased.

'Goosey!' whispered his mother, 'getting seepy? Is the sandman throwing sand in your eyes? Old Sandman at it? Sh—' ... He had gone.

Emmie took him. The women spoke in whispers. And Mrs Blackshaw, after a day spent in being a mother, reconstituted herself a wife, and began to beautify herself for her husband.

II

Yes, there was a Mr Blackshaw, and with Mr Blackshaw the tragedy of the bath commences. Mr Blackshaw was a very important young man. Indeed, it is within the mark to say that, next to his son, he was the most important young man in Bursley. For Mr Blackshaw was the manager of the newly opened Muncipal Electricity Works. And the Municipal Electricity had created more excitement and interest than anything since the 1887 Jubilee, when an ox was roasted whole in the market-place and turned bad in the process. Had Bursley been a Swiss village, or a French country town, or a hamlet in Arizona, it would have had its electricity fifteen years ago, but being only a progressive English Borough, with an annual value of a hundred and fifty thousand pounds, it struggled on with gas till well into the twentieth century. Its great neighbour Hanbridge had become acquainted with electricity in the nineteenth century.

All the principal streets and squares, and every decent shop that Hanbridge competition had left standing, and many private houses, now lighted themselves by electricity, and the result was splendid and glaring and coldly yellow. Mr. Blackshaw developed into the hero of the hour. People looked at him in the street as though he had been the discoverer and original maker of electricity. And if the manager of the gasworks had not already committed murder, it was because the manager of the gasworks had a right sense of what was due to his position as vicar's churchwarden at St Peter's Church.

But greatness has its penalties. And the chief penalty of Mr Blackshaw's greatness was that he could not see Roger have his nightly bath. It was impossible for Mr Blackshaw to quit his arduous and responsible post before seven o'clock in the evening. Later on, when things were going more smoothly, he might be able to get away; but then, later on, his son's bath would not be so amusing and agreeable as it then, by all reports, was. The baby was, of course, bathed on Saturday nights, but Sunday afternoon and evening Mr Blackshaw was obliged to spend with his invalid mother at Longshaw. It was on the sole condition of his weekly presence thus in her house that she had consented not to live with the married pair. And so Mr Blackshaw could not witness Roger's bath. He adored Roger. He understood Roger. He weighed, nursed, and fed Roger. He was 'up' in all the newest theories of infant rearing. In short, Roger was his passion, and he knew everything of Roger except Roger's bath. And when his wife met him at the front door of a night at seven-thirty and launched instantly into a description of the wonders, delights, and excitations of Roger's latest bath, Mr Blackshaw was ready to tear his hair with disappointment and frustration.

'I suppose you couldn't put it off for a couple of hours one night, May?' he suggested at supper on the evening of the particular bath described above.

'Sidney!' protested Mrs Blackshaw, pained.

Mr Blackshaw felt that he had gone too far, and there was a silence.

'Well!' said Mr Blackshaw at length, 'I have just made up my mind. I'm going to see that Kid's bath, and, what's more, I'm going to see it tomorrow. I don't care what happens.'

'But how shall you manage to get away, darling?'

'You will telephone me about a quarter of an hour before you're ready to begin, and I'll pretend it's something very urgent, and scoot off.'

'Well, that will be lovely, darling!' said Mrs Blackshaw. 'I WOULD like you to see him in the bath, just once! He looks so—'

And so on.

The next day, Mr Blackshaw, that fearsome autocrat of the Municipal Electricity Works, was saying to himself all day that at five o'clock he was going to assist at the spectacle of his wonderful son's bath. The prospect inspired him. So much so that every hand on the place was doing its utmost in fear and trembling, and the whole affair was running with the precision and smoothness of a watch.

From four o'clock onwards, Mr Blackshaw, in the solemn, illuminated privacy of the managerial office, safe behind glass partitions, could no more contain his excitement. He hovered in front of the telephone, waiting for it to ring. Then, at a quarter to five, just when he felt he couldn't stand it any longer, and was about to ring up his wife instead of waiting for her to ring him up, he saw a burly shadow behind the glass door, and gave a desolate sigh. That shadow could only be thrown by one person, and that person was his Worship the Mayor of Bursley. His Worship entered the private office with mayoral assurance, pulling in his wake a stout old lady whom he introduced as his aunt from Wolverhampton. And he calmly proposed that Mr Blackshaw should show the mayoral aunt over the new Electricity Works!

Mr Blackshaw was sick of showing people over the Works. Moreover, he naturally despised the Mayor. All permanent officials of municipalities thoroughly despise their mayors (up their sleeves). A mayor is here today and gone tomorrow, whereas a permanent official is permanent. A mayor knows nothing about anything except his chain and the rules of debate, and he is, further, a tedious and meddlesome person—in the opinion of permanent officials.

So Mr Blackshaw's fury at the inept appearance of the Mayor and the mayoral aunt at this critical juncture may be imagined. The worst of it was, he didn't know how to refuse the Mayor.

Then the telephone-bell rang.

'Excuse me,' said Mr Blackshaw, with admirably simulated politeness, going to the instrument. 'Are you there? Who is it?'

'It's me, darling,' came the thin voice of his wife far away at Bleakridge. 'The water's just getting hot. We're nearly ready. Can you come now?'

'By Jove! Wait a moment!' exclaimed Mr Blackshaw, and then turning to his visitors, 'Did you hear that?'

'No,' said the Mayor.

'All those three new dynamos that they've got at the Hanbridge Electricity Works have just broken down. I knew they would. I told them they would!'

'Dear, dear!' said the Mayor of Bursley, secretly delighted by this disaster to a disdainful rival. 'Why! They'll have the town in darkness. What are they going to do?'

'They want me to go over at once. But, of course, I can't. At least, I must give myself the pleasure of showing you and this lady over our Works, first.'

'Nothing of the kind, Mr Blackshaw!' said the Mayor. 'Go at once. Go at once. If Bursley can be of any assistance to Hanbridge in such a crisis, I shall be only too pleased. We will come tomorrow, won't we, auntie?'

Mr Blackshaw addressed the telephone.

'The Mayor is here, with a lady, and I was just about to show them over the Works, but his Worship insists that I come at once.'

'Certainly,' the Mayor put in pompously.

'Wonders will never cease,' came the thin voice of Mrs Blackshaw through the telephone. 'It's very nice of the old thing! What's his lady friend like?'

'Not like anything. Unique!' replied Mr Blackshaw.

'Young?' came the voice.

'Dates from the thirties,' said Mr Blackshaw. 'I'm coming.' And rang off.

'I didn't know there was any electric machinery as old as that,' said the mayoral aunt.

'We'll just look about us a bit,' the Mayor remarked. 'Don't lose a moment, Mr Blackshaw.'

And Mr Blackshaw hurried off, wondering vaguely how he should explain the lie when it was found out, but not caring much. After all, he could easily ascribe the episode to the trick of some practical joker.

III

He arrived at his commodious and electrically lit residence in the very nick of time, and full to overflowing with innocent paternal glee. Was he not about to see Roger's tub? Roger was just ready to be carried upstairs as Mr Blackshaw's latchkey turned in the door.

'Wait a sec!' cried Mr Blackshaw to his wife, who had the child in her arms, 'I'll carry him up.'

And he threw away his hat, stick, and overcoat and grabbed ecstatically at the infant. And he had got perhaps halfway up the stairs, when lo! the electric light went out. Every electric light in the house went out.

'Great Scott!' breathed Mr Blackshaw, aghast.

He pulled aside the blind of the window at the turn of the stairs, and peered forth. The street was as black as your hat, or nearly so.

'Great Scott!' he repeated. 'May, get candles.'

Something had evidently gone wrong at the Works. Just his luck! He had quitted the Works for a quarter of an hour, and the current had failed!

Of course, the entire house was instantly in an uproar, turned upside down, startled out of its life. But a few candles soon calmed its transports. And at length Mr Blackshaw gained the bedroom in safety, with the offspring of his desires comfortable in a shawl.

'Give him to me,' said May shortly. 'I suppose you'll have to go back to the Works at once?'

Mr Blackshaw paused, and then nerved himself; but while he was pausing, May, glancing at the two feeble candles, remarked: 'It's very tiresome. I'm sure I shan't be able to see properly.'

'No!' almost shouted Mr Blackshaw. 'I'll watch this kid have his bath or I'll die for it! I don't care if all the Five Towns are in darkness. I don't care if the Mayor's aunt has got caught in a dynamo and is suffering horrible tortures. I've come to see this bath business, and dashed if I don't see it!'

'Well, don't stand between the bath and the fire, dearest,' said May coldly.

Meanwhile, Emmie, having pretty nearly filled the bath with a combination of hot and cold waters, dropped the floating thermometer into it, and then added more waters until the thermometer indicated the precise temperature proper for a baby's bath. But you are not to imagine that Mrs Blackshaw trusted a thermometer—

She did not, however, thrust her bared arm into the water this time. No! Roger, who never cried before his bath, was crying, was indubitably crying. And he cried louder and louder.

'Stand where he can't see you, dearest. He isn't used to you at bath-time,' said Mrs Blackshaw still coldly. 'Are you, my pet? There! There!'

Mr Blackshaw effaced himself, feeling a fool. But Roger continued to cry. He cried himself purple. He cried till the veins stood out on his forehead and his mouth was like a map of Australia. He cried himself into a monster of ugliness. Neither mother nor nurse could do anything with him at all.

'I think you've upset him, dearest,' said Mrs Blackshaw even more coldly. 'Hadn't you better go?'

'Well—' protested the father.

'I think you had better go,' said Mrs Blackshaw, adding no term of endearment, and visibly controlling herself with difficulty.

And Mr Blackshaw went. He had to go. He went out into the unelectric night. He headed for the Works, not because he cared twopence, at that moment, about the accident at the Works, whatever it was; but simply because the Works was the only place to go to. And even outside in the dark street he could hear the rousing accents of his progeny.

People were talking to each other as they groped about in the road, and either making jokes at the expense of the new Electricity Department, or frankly cursing it with true Five Towns directness of speech. And as Mr Blackshaw went down the hill into the town his heart was as black as the street itself with rage and disappointment. He had made his child cry!

Someone stopped him.

'Eh, Mester Blackshaw!' said a voice, and under the voice a hand struck a match to light a pipe. 'What's th' maning o' this eclipse as you'm treating us to?'

Mr Blackshaw looked right through the inquirer—a way he had when his brain was working hard. And he suddenly smiled by the light of the match.

'That child wasn't crying because I was there,' said Mr Blackshaw with solemn relief. 'Not at all! He was crying because he didn't understand the candles. He isn't used to candles, and they frightened him.'

And he began to hurry towards the Works.

At the same instant the electric light returned to Bursley. The current was resumed.

'That's better,' said Mr Blackshaw, sighing.

THE SILENT BROTHERS

I

John and Robert Hessian, brothers, bachelors, and dressed in mourning, sat together after supper in the parlour of their house at the bottom of Oldcastle Street, Bursley. Maggie, the middle- aged servant, was clearing the table.

'Leave the cloth and the coffee,' said John, the elder, 'Mr Liversage is coming in.'

'Yes, Mr John,' said Maggie.

'Slate, Maggie,' Robert ordered laconically, with a gesture towards the mantelpiece behind him.

'Yes, Mr Robert,' said Maggie.

She gave him a slate with slate-pencil attached, which hung on a nail near the mantlepiece.

Robert took the slate and wrote on it: 'What is Liversage coming about?'

And he pushed the slate across the table to John.

Whereupon John wrote on the slate: 'Don't know. He telephoned me he wanted to see us tonight.'

And he pushed back the slate to Robert.

This singular procedure was not in the least attributable to deafness on the part of the brothers; they were in the prime of life, aged forty-two and thirty-nine respectively, and in complete possession of all their faculties. It was due simply to the fact that they had quarrelled, and would not speak to each other. The history of their quarrel would be incredible were it not full of that ridiculous pathetic quality known as human nature, and did not similar things happen frequently in the manufacturing Midlands, where the general temperament is a fearful and strange compound of pride, obstinacy, unconquerableness, romance, and stupidity. Yes, stupidity.

No single word had passed between the brothers in that house for ten years. On the morning after the historical quarrel Robert had not replied when John spoke to him. 'Well,' said John's secret heart—and John's secret heart ought to have known better, as it was older than its brother heart—'I'll teach him a lesson. I won't speak until he does.' And Robert's secret heart had somehow divined this idiotic resolution, and had said: 'We shall see.' Maggie had been the first to notice the stubborn silence. Then their friends noticed it, especially Mr Liversage, the solicitor, their most intimate friend. But you are not to suppose that anybody protested very strongly. For John and Robert were not the kind of men with whom liberties may be taken; and, moreover, Bursley was slightly amused—at the beginning. It assumed the attitude of a disinterested spectator at a fight. It wondered who would win. Of course, it called both the brothers fools, yet in a tone somewhat sympathetic, because such a thing as had occurred to the Hessians might well occur to any man gifted with the true Bursley spirit. There is this to be said for a Bursley man: Having made his bed, he will lie on it, and he will not complain.

The Hessians suffered severely by their self-imposed dumbness, but they suffered like Stoics. Maggie also suffered, and Maggie would not stand it. Maggie it was who had invented the slate. Indeed, they had heard some plain truths from that stout, bustling woman. They had not yielded, but they had accepted the slate in order to minimize the inconvenience to Maggie, and afterwards they deigned to make use of it for their own purposes. As for friends—friends accustomed themselves to the status quo. There came a time when the spectacle of two men chattering to everybody else in a company, and not saying a word to each other, no longer appealed to Bursley's sense of humour. The silent scenes at which Maggie assisted every day did not, either, appeal to Maggie's sense of humour, because she had none. So the famous feud grew into a sort of elemental fact of Nature. It was tolerated as the weather is tolerated. The brothers acquired pride in it; even Bursley regarded it as an interesting municipal curiosity. The sole imperfection in a lovely and otherwise perfect quarrel was that John and Robert, being both employed at Roycroft's Majolica Manufactory, the one as works manager and the other as commercial traveller, were obliged to speak to each other occasionally in the way of business. Artistically, this was a pity, though they did speak very sternly and distantly. The partial truce necessitated by Roycroft's was confined strictly to Roycroft's. And when Robert was not on his journeys, these two tall, strong, dark, bearded men might often be seen of a night walking separately and doggedly down Oldcastle Street from the works, within five yards of each other.

And no one suggested the lunatic asylum. Such is the force of pride, of rank stupidity, and of habit.

The slate-scratching was scarcely over that evening when Mr Powell Liversage appeared. He was a golden-haired man, with a jolly face, lighter and shorter in structure than the two brothers. His friendship with them dated from school-days, and it had survived even the entrance of Liversage into a learned profession. Liversage, who, being a bachelor like the Hessians, had many unoccupied evenings, came to see the brothers regularly every Saturday night, and one or other of them dropped in upon him most Wednesdays; but this particular night was a Thursday.

'How do?' John greeted him succinctly between two puffs of a pipe.

'How do?' replied Liversage.

'How do, Pow?' Robert greeted him in turn, also between two puffs of a pipe.

And 'How do, little 'un?' replied Liversage.

A chair was indicated to him, and he sat down, and Robert poured out some coffee into a third cup which Maggie had brought. John pushed away the extra special of the Staffordshire Signal, which he had been reading.

'What's up these days?' John demanded.

'Well,' said Liversage, and both brothers noticed that he was rather ill at ease, instead of being humorous and lightly caustic as usual, 'the will's turned up.'

'The devil it has!' John exclaimed. 'When?'

'This afternoon.'

And then, as there was a pause, Liversage added: 'Yes, my sons, the will's turned up.'

'But where, you cuckoo, sitting there like that?' asked Robert. 'Where?'

'It was in that registered letter addressed to your sister that the Post Office people wouldn't hand over until we'd taken out letters of administration.'

'Well, I'm dashed!' muttered John. 'Who'd have thought of that? You've got the will, then?'

Liversage nodded.

The Hessians had an elder sister, Mrs Bott, widow of a colour merchant, and Mrs Bott had died suddenly three months ago, the night after a journey to Manchester. (Even at the funeral the brothers had scandalized the town by not speaking to each other.) Mrs Bott had wealth, wit, and wisdom, together with certain peculiarities, of which one was an excessive secrecy. It was known that she had made a will, because she had more than once notified the fact, in a tone suggestive of highly important issues, but the will had refused to be found. So Mr Liversage had been instructed to take out letters of administration of the estate, which, in the continued absence of the will, would be divided equally between the brothers. And twelve or thirteen thousand pounds may be compared to a financial beef-steak that cuts up very handsomely for two persons. The carving-knife was about to descend on its succulence, when, lo! the will!

'How came the will to be in the post?' asked Robert.

'The handwriting on the envelope was your sister's,' said Liversage. 'And the package was posted in Manchester. Very probably she had taken the will to Manchester to show it to a lawyer or something of that sort, and then she was afraid of losing it on the journey back, and so she sent it to herself by registered post. But before it arrived, of course, she was dead.'

'That wasn't a bad scheme of poor Mary Ann's!' John commented.

'It was just like her!' said Robert, speaking pointedly to Liversage. 'But what an odd thing!'

Now, both these men were, no doubt excusably, agonized by curiosity to learn the contents of the will. But would either of them be the first to express that curiosity? Never in this world! Not for the fortune itself! To do so would scarcely have been Bursleyish. It would certainly not have been Hessianlike. So Liversage was obliged at length to say—

'I reckon I'd better read you the will, eh?'

The brothers nodded.

'Mind you,' said Liversage, 'it's not my will. I've had nothing to do with it; so kindly keep your hair on. As a matter of fact, she must have drawn it up herself. It's not drawn properly at all, but it's witnessed all right, and it'll hold water, just as well as if the blooming Lord Chancellor had fixed it up for her in person.'

He produced the document and read, awkwardly and self- consciously—

'"This is my will. You are both of you extremely foolish, John and Robert, and I've often told you so. Nobody has ever understood, and nobody ever will understand, why you quarrelled like that over Annie Emery. You are punishing yourselves, but you are punishing her as well, and it isn't fair her waiting all these years. So I give all my estate, no matter what it is, to whichever of you marries Annie. And I hope this will teach you a lesson. You need it more than you need my money. But you must be married within a year of my death. And if the one that marries cares to give five thousand pounds or so to the other, of course there's nothing to prevent him. This is just a hint. And if you don't either of you marry Annie within a year, then I just leave everything I have to Miss Annie Emery (spinster), stationer and fancy-goods dealer, Duck Bank, Bursley. She deserves something for her disappointment, and she shall have it. Mr Liversage, solicitor, must kindly be my executor. And I commit my soul to God, hoping for a blessed resurrection. 20th January, 1896. Signed Mary Ann Bott, widow." As I told you, the witnessing is in order,' Liversage finished.

'Give it here,' said John shortly, and scanned the sheet of paper.

And Robert actually walked round the table and looked over his brother's shoulder—ample proof that he was terrifically moved.

'And do you mean to tell me that a will like that is good in law?' exclaimed John.

'Of course it's good in law!' Liversage replied. 'Legal phraseology is a useful thing, and it often saves trouble in the end; but it ain't indispensable, you know.'

'Humph!' was Robert's comment as he resumed his seat and relighted his pipe.

All three men were nervous. Each was afraid to speak, afraid even to meet the eyes of the other two. An unmajestic silence followed.

'Well, I'll be off, I think,' Liversage remarked at length with difficulty.

He rose.

'I say,' Robert stopped him. 'Better not say anything about this to Miss—to Annie, eh?'

'I will say nothing,' agreed Liversage (infamously and unprofessionally concealing the fact that he had already said something).

And he departed.

The brothers sat in flustered meditation over the past and the future.

Ten years before, Annie Emery had been an orphan of twenty-three, bravely starting in business for herself amid the plaudits of the admiring town; and John had fallen in love with her courage and her sense and her feminine charm. But alas, as Ovid points out, how difficult it is for a woman to please only one man! Robert also had fallen in love with Annie. Each brother had accused the other of underhand and unbrotherly practices in the pursuit of Annie. Each was profoundly hurt by the accusations, and each, in the immense fatuity of his pride, had privately sworn to prove his innocence by having nothing more to do with Annie. Such is life! Such is man! Such is the terrible egoism of man! And thus it was that, for the sake of wounded pride, John and Robert not only did not speak to one another for ten years, but they spoilt at least one of their lives; and they behaved ignobly to Annie, who would certainly have married either one or the other of them.

At two o'clock in the morning John pulled a coin out of his pocket and made the gesture of tossing.

'Who shall go first!' he explained.

Robert had a queer sensation in his spine as his elder brother spoke to him for the first time in ten years. He wanted to reply vocally. He had a most imperious desire to reply vocally. But he could not. Something stronger even than the desire prevented his tongue from moving.

John tossed the coin—it was a sovereign—and covered it with his hands.

'Tail!' Robert murmured, somewhat hoarsely.

But it was head.

Then they went to bed.

II

The side door of Miss Emery's shop was in Brick Passage, and not in the main street, so that a man, even a man of commanding stature and formidable appearance, might by insinuating himself into Brick Street, off King Street, and then taking the passage from the quieter end, arrive at it without attracting too much attention. This course was adopted by John Hessian. From the moment when he quitted his own house that Friday evening in June he had been subject to the delusion that the collective eye of Bursley was upon him. As a matter of fact, the collective eye of Bursley is much too large and important to occupy itself exclusively with a single individual. Bursley is not a village, and let no one think it. Nevertheless, John was subject to the delusion.

The shop was shut, as he knew it would be. But the curtained window of the parlour, between the side-door and the small shuttered side-window of the shop, gave a strange suggestion of interesting virgin spotless domesticity within. John cast a fearful eye on the main thoroughfare. Nobody seemed to be passing. The chapel-keeper of the Wesleyan Chapel on the opposite side of Trafalgar Road was refreshing the massive Corinthian portico of that fane, and paying no regard whatever to the temple of Eros which Miss Emery's shop had suddenly become.

So John knocked.

'I am a fool!' his thought ran as he knocked.

Because he did not know what he was about. He had won the toss, and with it the right to approach Annie Emery before his brother. But what then? Well, he did desire to marry her, quite as much for herself as for his sister's fortune. But what then? How was he going to explain the tepidity, the desertion, the long sin against love of ten years? In short, how was he going to explain the inexplicable? He could decidedly do nothing that evening except make a blundering ass of himself. And how soon would Robert have the right to come along and say HIS say? That point had not been settled. Points so extremely delicate cannot be settled on a slate, and he had not dared to broach it viva voce to his younger brother. He had been too afraid of a rebuff.

He then hoped that Annie's servant would tell him that Annie was out.

Annie, however, took him at a disadvantage by opening the door herself.

'Well, MR HESSIAN!' she exclaimed, her face bursting into a swift and welcoming smile.

'I was just passing,' the donkey in him blundered forth. 'And I thought—'

However, in fifteen seconds he was on the domestic side of the sitting-room window, and seated in the antimacassared armchair between the fire-place and the piano, and Annie had taken his hat and told him that her servant was out for the evening.

'But I'm disturbing your supper, Miss Emery,' he said. Flurried though he was, he could not fail to notice the white embroidered cloth spread diagonally on the table, and the cold meat and the pastry and the glittering cutlery and crystal thereon.

'Not at all,' she replied. 'You haven't had supper yet, I expect?'

'No,' he said, not thinking.

'It will be nice of you to help me to eat mine,' said she.

'Oh! But really—'

But she got plates and things out of the cupboard below the bookcase—and there he was! She would take no refusal. It was wondrous.

'I'm awfully glad I came now,' his thought ran; I'm managing it rather well.'

And—

'Poor Bob!'

His sole discomfort was that he could not invent a sufficiently ingenious explanation of his call. You can't tell a woman you've called to make love to her, and when your previous call happens to have been ten years ago, some kind of an explanation does seem to be demanded. Ultimately, as Annie was so very pleased to see him, so friendly, so feminine, so equal to the occasion, he decided to let his presence in her abode that night stand as one of those central facts in existence that need no explanation. And they went on talking and eating till the dusk deepened and Annie lit the gas and drew the blind.

He watched her on the sly as she moved about the room. He decided that she did not appear a day older. There was the same plump, erect figure, the same neatness, the same fair skin and fair hair, the same little nose, the same twinkle in the eye—only perhaps the twinkle in the eye was a trifle less cruel than it used to be. She was not a day older. (In this he was of course utterly mistaken; she was ten years older, she was thirty-three, with ten years of successful commercial experience behind her; she would never be twenty-three again. Still she was a most desirable woman, and a woman infinitely beyond his deserts.) Her air of general capability impressed him. And with that there was mingled a strange softness, a marvellous hint of a concealed wish to surrender.... Well, she made him feel big and masculine—in brief, a man.

He regretted the lost ten years. His present way of life seemed intolerable to him. The new heaven opened its gate and gave glimpses of paradise. After all, he felt himself well qualified for that paradise. He felt that he had all along been a woman's man, without knowing it.

'By Jove!' his thought ran. 'At this rate I might propose to her in a week or two.'

And again—

'Poor old Bobbie!'

A quarter of an hour later, in some miraculous manner, they were more intimate than they had ever been, much more intimate. He revised his estimate of the time that must elapse before he might propose to her. In another five minutes he was fighting hard against a mad impulse to propose to her on the spot. And then the fight was over, and he had lost. He proposed to her under the rose-coloured shade of the Welsbach light.

She drew away, as though shot.

And with the rapidity of lightning, in the silence which followed, he went back to his original criticism of himself, that he was a fool. Naturally she would request him to leave. She would accuse him of effrontery.

Her lips trembled. He prepared to rise.

'It's so sudden!' she said.

Bliss! Glory! Celestial joy! Her words were at least equivalent to an absolution of his effrontery! She would accept! She would accept! He jumped up and approached her. But she jumped up too and retreated. He was not to win his prize so easily.

'Please sit down,' she murmured. 'I must think it over,' she said, apparently mastering herself. 'Shall you be at chapel next Sunday morning?'

'Yes,' he answered.

'If I am there, and if I am wearing white roses in my hat, it will mean—' She dropped her eyes.

'Yes?' he queried.

And she nodded.

'And supposing you aren't there?'

'Then the Sunday after,' she said.

He thanked her in his Hessian style.

'I prefer that way of telling you,' she smiled demurely. 'It will avoid the necessity for another—so much—you understand?...'

'Quite so, quite so!' he agreed. 'I quite understand.'

'And if I DO see those roses,' he went on, 'I shall take upon myself to drop in for tea, may I?'

She paused.

'In any case, you mustn't speak to me coming out of chapel, PLEASE.'

As he walked home down Oldcastle Street he said to himself that the age of miracles was not past; also that, after all, he was not so old as the tale of his years would mathematically indicate.

III

Her absence from chapel on the next Sunday disagreed with him. However, Robert was away nearly all the week, and he had the house to himself to dream in. It frequently happened to him to pass by Miss Emery's shop, but he caught no glimpse of her, and though he really was in serious need of writing-paper and envelopes, he dared not enter. Robert returned on the Friday.

On the morning of the second Sunday, John got up early, in order to cope with a new necktie that he had purchased in Hanbridge. Nevertheless he found Robert afoot before him, and Robert, by some unlucky chance, was wearing not merely a new necktie, but a new suit of clothes. They breakfasted in their usual august silence, and John gathered from a remark of Robert's to Maggie when she brought in the boots that Robert meant to go to chapel. Now, Robert, being a commercial traveller and therefore a bit of a caution, did not attend chapel with any remarkable assiduity. And John, in the privacy of his own mind, blamed him for having been so clumsy as to choose that particular morning for breaking the habits of a lifetime. Still, the presence of Robert in the pew could not prejudicially affect John, and so there was no genuine cause for gloominess.

After a time it became apparent that each was waiting for the other to go. John began to get annoyed. At last he made the plunge and went. Turning his head halfway up Oldcastle Street, opposite the mansion which is called 'Miss Peel's', he perceived Robert fifty yards behind. It was a glorious June day.

He blushed as he entered chapel. If he was nervous, it may be accorded to him as excuse that the happiness of his life depended on what he should see within the next few minutes. However, he felt pretty sure, though it was exciting all the same.

To reach the Hessian pew he was obliged to pass Miss Emery's. And it was empty! Robert arrived.

The organist finished the voluntary. The leading tenor of the choir put up the number of the first hymn. The minister ascended the staircase of the great mahogany pulpit, and prayed silently, and arranged his papers in the leaves of the hymn-book, and glanced about to see who was there and who was presumably still in bed, and coughed; and then Miss Annie Emery sailed in with that air of false calm which is worn by the experienced traveller who catches a train by the fifth of a second. The service commenced.

John looked.

She was wearing white roses. There could be no mistake as to that. There were about a hundred and fifty-five white roses in the garden of her hat.

What a thrill ran through John's heart! He had won Annie, and he had won the fortune. Yes, he would give Robert the odd five thousand pounds. His state of mind might even lead him to make it guineas. He heard not a word of the sermon, and throughout the service he rose up and sat down several instants after the rest of the congregation, because he was so absent-minded.

After service he waited for everybody else to leave, in order not to break his promise to the divine Annie. So did Robert. This ill- timed rudeness on Robert's part somewhat retarded the growth of a young desire in John's heart to make friends with poor Bob. Then he got up and left, and Robert followed.

They dined in silence, John deciding that he would begin his overtures of friendship after he had seen Annie, and could tell Robert that he was formally engaged. The brothers ate little. They both improved their minds during their repast—John with the Christian Commonwealth, and Robert with the Saturday cricket edition of the Signal (I regret it).

Then, after pipes, they both went out for a walk, naturally not in the same direction. The magnificence of the weather filled them both with the joy of life. As for John, he went out for a walk simply because he could not contain himself within the house. He could not wait immovable till four-thirty, the hour at which he meant to call on Annie for tea and the betrothal kiss. Therefore he ascended to Hillport and wandered as far as Oldcastle, all in a silk hat and a frock-coat.

It was precisely half-past four as he turned, unassumingly, from Brick Street into Brick Passage, and so approached the side door of Annie Emery's. And his astonishment and anger were immense when he saw Robert, likewise in silk hat and frock-coat, penetrating into Brick Passage from the other end.

They met, and their inflamed spirits collided.

'What's the meaning of this?' John demanded, furious; and, simultaneously, Robert demanded: 'What in Hades are YOU doing here?'

Only Sunday and the fine clothes and the proximity to Annie prevented actual warfare.

'I'm calling on Annie,' said John.

'So am I,' said Robert.

'Well, you're too late,' said John.

'Oh, I'm too late, am I?' said Robert, with a disdainful laugh. Thanks!'

'I tell you you're too late,' said John. 'You may as well know at once that I've proposed to Annie and she's accepted me.'

'I like that! I like that!' said Robert.

'Don't shout!' said John.

'I'm not shouting,' said Robert. 'But you may as well know that you're mistaken, my boy. It's me that's proposed to Annie and been accepted. You must be off your chump.'

'When did you propose to her?' said John.

'On Friday, if you must know,' said Robert.

'And she accepted you at once?' said John.

'No. She said that if she was wearing white roses in her hat this morning at chapel, that would mean she accepted,' said Robert.

'Liar!' said John.

'I suppose you'll admit she WAS wearing white roses in her hat?' said Robert, controlling himself.

'Liar!' said John, and continued breathless: 'That was what she said to ME. She must have told you that white roses meant a refusal.'

'Oh no, she didn't!' said Robert, quailing secretly, but keeping up a formidable show of courage. 'You're an old fool!' he added vindictively.

They were both breathing hard, and staring hard at each other.

'Come away,' said John. 'Come away! We can't talk here. She may look out of the window.'

So they went away. They walked very quickly home, and, once in the parlour, they began to have it out. And, before they had done, the reading of cricket news on Sunday was as nothing compared to the desecrating iniquity which they committed. The scene was not such as can be decently recounted. But about six o'clock Maggie entered, and, at considerable personal risk, brought them back to a sense of what was due to their name, the town, and the day. She then stated that she would not remain in such a house, and she departed.

IV

'But whatever made you do it, dearest?'

These words were addressed to Annie Emery on the glorious summer evening which closed that glorious summer day, and they were addressed to her by no other person than Powell Liversage. The pair were in the garden of the house in Trafalgar Road occupied by Mr Liversage and his mother, and they looked westwards over the distant ridge of Hillport, where the moon was setting.

'Whatever made me do it!' repeated Annie, and the twinkle in her eye had that charming cruelty which John had missed. 'Did they not deserve it? Of course, I can talk to you now with perfect freedom, can't I? Well, what do you THINK of it? Here for ten years neither one nor the other does more than recognize me in the street, and then all of a sudden they come down on me like that—simply because there's a question of money. I couldn't have believed men could be so stupid—no, I really couldn't! They're friends of yours, Powell, I know, but—however, that's no matter. But it was too ridiculously easy to lead them on! They'd swallow any flattery. I just did it to see what they'd do, and I think I arranged it pretty well. I quite expected they would call about the same time, and then shouldn't I have given them my mind! Unfortunately they met outside, and got very hot—I saw them from the bedroom window—and went away.'

'You mustn't forget, my dear girl,' said Liversage, 'that it was you they quarrelled about. I don't want to defend 'em for a minute, but it wasn't altogether the money that sent them to you; it was more that the money gave them an excuse for coming!'

'It was a very bad excuse, then!' said Annie.

'Agreed!' Liversage murmured.

The moon was extremely lovely and romantic against the distant spire of Hillport Church, and its effect on the couple was just what might have been anticipated.

'Perhaps I'm sorry,' Annie admitted at length, with a charming grimace.

'Oh! I don't think there's anything to be SORRY about,' said Liversage. 'But of course they'll think I've had a hand in it. You see, I've never breathed a word to them about—about my feelings towards you.'

'No?'

'No. It would have been rather a delicate subject, you see, with them. And I'm sure they'll be staggered when they know that we got engaged last night. They'll certainly say I've—er—been after you for the—No, they won't. They're decent chaps, really; very decent.'

'Anyhow, you may be sure, dear,' said Annie stiffly, 'that *I* shan't rob them of their vile money! Nothing would induce me to touch it!'

'Of course not, dearest!' said Liversage—or, rather the finer part of him said it; the baser part somewhat regretted that vile twelve thousand or so. (I must be truthful.)

He took her hand again.

At the same moment old Mrs Liversage came hastening down the garden, and Liversage dropped the hand.

'Powell,' she said. 'Here's John Hessian, and he wants to see you!'

'The dickens!' exclaimed Liversage, glancing at Annie.

'I must go,' said Annie. 'I shall go by the fields. Good night, dear Mrs Liversage.'

'Wait ten seconds,' Liversage pleaded, 'and I'll be with you.' And he ran off.

John, haggard and undone, was awaiting him in the drawing-room.

'Pow,' said he, 'I've had a fearful row with Bob, and I can't possibly sleep in our house tonight. Don't talk to me. But let me have one of the beds in your spare room, will you? There's a good chap.'

'Why, of course, Johnnie,' said Liversage. 'Of course.'

'And I'll go right to bed now,' said John.

An hour later, after Powell Liversage had seen his affianced to her abode and returned home, and after his mother had gone to bed, there was a knock at the front door, and Liversage opened to Robert Hessian.

'Look here, Pow,' said Robert, whose condition was deplorable, 'I want to sleep here tonight. Do you mind? Fact is, I've had a devil of a shindy with Jack, and Maggie's run off, and, anyhow, I couldn't possibly stop in the same house with Jack tonight.'

'But what—?'

'See here,' said Robert. 'I can't talk. Just let me have a bed in your spare room. I'm sure you mother won't mind.'

'Why, certainly,' said Liversage.

He lit a candle, escorted Robert upstairs, opened the door of the spare room, gave the candle to Robert, pushed him in, said 'Good night,' and shut the door.

What a night!

THE NINETEENTH HAT

A dramatic moment was about to arrive in the joint career of Stephen Cheswardine and Vera his wife. The motor-car stood by the side of the pavement of the Strand, Torquay, that resort of southern wealth and fashion. The chauffeur, Felix, had gone into the automobile shop to procure petrol. Mr Cheswardine looking longer than ever in his long coat, was pacing the busy footpath. Mrs Cheswardine, her beauty obscured behind a flowing brown veil, was lolling in the tonneau, very pleased to be in the tonneau, very pleased to be observed by all Torquay in the tonneau, very satisfied with her husband, and with the Napier car, and especially with Felix, now buying petrol. Suddenly Mrs Cheswardine perceived that next door but one to the automobile shop was a milliner's. She sat up and gazed. According to a card in the window an 'after-season sale' was in progress that June day at the milliner's. There were two rows of hats in the window, each hat plainly ticketed. Mrs Cheswardine descended from the car, crossed the pavement, and gave to the window the whole of her attention.

She sniffed at most of the hats. But one of them, of green straw, with a large curving green wing on either side of the crown, and a few odd bits of fluffiness here and there, pleased her. It was Parisian. She had been to Paris—once. An 'after-season' sale at a little shop in Torquay would not, perhaps, seem the most likely place in the world to obtain a chic hat; it is, moreover, a notorious fact that really chic hats cannot be got for less than three pounds, and this hat was marked ten shillings. Nevertheless, hats are most mysterious things. Their quality of being chic is more often the fruit of chance than of design, particularly in England. You never know when nor where you may light on a good hat. Vera considered that she had lighted on one.

'They're probably duck's feathers dyed,' she said to herself. 'But it's a darling of a hat and it will suit me to a T.'

As for the price, when once you have taken the ticket off a hat the secret of its price is gone forever. Many a hat less smart than this hat has been marked in Bond Street at ten guineas instead of ten shillings. Hats are like oil-paintings—they are worth what people will give for them.

So Vera approached her husband, and said, with an enchanting, innocent smile—

'Lend me half-a-sovereign, will you, doggie?'

She called him doggie in those days because he was a sort of dog- man, a sort of St Bernard, shaggy and big, with faithful eyes; and he enjoyed being called doggie.

But on this occasion he was not to be bewitched by the enchanting innocence of the smile nor by the endearing epithet. He refused to relax his features.

'You aren't going to buy another hat, are you?' he asked sternly, challengingly.

The smile disappeared from her face, and she pulled her slim young self together.

'Yes,' she replied harshly.

The battle was definitely engaged. You may inquire why a man financially capable of hiring a 20-24 h.p. Napier car, with a French chauffeur named Felix, for a week or more, should grudge his wife ten shillings for a hat. Well, you are to comprehend that it was not a question of ten shillings, it was a question of principle. Vera already had eighteen hats, and it had been clearly understood between them that no more money should be spent on attire for quite a long time. Vera was entirely in the wrong. She knew it, and he knew it. But she wanted just that hat.

And they were on their honeymoon, you know: which enormously intensified the poignancy of the drama. They had been married only six days; in three days more they were to return to the Five Towns, where Stephen was solidly established as an earthenware manufacturer. You who have been through them are aware what ticklish things honeymoons are, and how much depends on the tactfulness of the more tactful of the two parties. Stephen, thirteen years older than Vera, was the more tactful of the two parties. He had married a beautiful and elegant woman, with vast unexploited capacities for love in her heart. But he had married a capricious woman, and he knew it. So far he had yielded to her caprices, as well became him; but in the depths of his masculine mind he had his own private notion as to the identity of the person who should ultimately be master in their house, and he had decided only the previous night that when the next moment for being firm arrived, firm he would be.

And now the moment was upon him. It was their eyes that fought, silently, bitterly. There is a great deal of bitterness in true love.

Stephen perceived the affair broadly, in all its aspects. He was older and much more experienced than Vera, and therefore he was responsible for the domestic peace, and for her happiness, and for his own, and for appearances, and for various other things. He perceived the moral degradation which would be involved in an open quarrel during the honeymoon. He perceived the difficulties of a battle in the street, in such a select and prim street as the Strand, Torquay, where the very backbone of England's respectability goes shopping. He perceived Vera's vast ignorance of life. He perceived her charm, and her naughtiness, and all her defects. And he perceived, further, that, this being the first conflict of their married existence, it was of the highest importance that he should emerge from it the victor. To allow Vera to triumph would gravely menace their future tranquillity and multiply the difficulties which her adorable capriciousness would surely cause. He could not afford to let her win. It was his duty, not merely to himself but to her, to conquer. But, on the other hand, he had never fully tested her powers of sheer obstinacy, her willingness to sacrifice everything for the satisfaction of a whim; and he feared these powers. He had a dim suspicion that Vera was one of that innumerable class of charming persons who are perfectly delicious and perfectly sweet so long as they have precisely their own way—and no longer.

Vera perceived only two things. She perceived the hat—although her back was turned towards it—and she perceived the half- sovereign—although it was hidden in Stephen's pocket.

'But, my dear,' Stephen protested, 'you know—'

'Will you lend me half-a-sovereign?' Vera repeated, in a glacial tone. The madness of a desired hat had seized her. She was a changed Vera. She was not a loving woman, not a duteous young wife, nor a reasoning creature. She was an embodied instinct for hats.

'It was most distinctly agreed,' Stephen murmured, restraining his anger.

Just then Felix came out of the shop, followed by a procession of three men bearing cans of petrol. If Stephen was Napoleon and Vera Wellington, Felix was the Blucher of this deplorable altercation. Impossible to have a row—yes, a row—with your wife in the presence of your chauffeur, with his French ideas of chivalry.

'Will you lend me half-a-sovereign?' Vera reiterated, in the same glacial tone, not caring twopence for the presence of Felix.

And Stephen, by means of an interminable silver chain, drew his sovereign-case from the profundity of his hip-pocket; it was like drawing a bucket out of a well. And he gave Vera half-a- sovereign; and THAT was like knotting the rope for his own execution.

And while Felix and his three men poured gallons and gallons of petrol into a hole under the cushions of the tonneau, Stephen swallowed his wrath on the pavement, and Vera remained hidden in the shop. And the men were paid and went off, and Felix took his seat ready to start. And then Vera came out of the hat place, and the new green hat was on her head, and the old one in a bag in her pretty hands.

'What do you think of my new hat, Felix?' she smiled to the favoured chauffeur; 'I hope it pleases you.'

Felix said that it did.

In these days, chauffeurs are a great race and a privileged. They have usurped the position formerly held by military officers. Women fawn on them, take fancies to them, and spoil them. They can do no wrong in the eyes of the sex. Vera had taken a fancy to Felix. Perhaps it was because he had been in a cavalry regiment; perhaps it was merely the curve of his moustache. Who knows? And Felix treated her as only a Frenchman can treat a pretty woman, with a sort of daring humility, with worship—in short, with true Gallic appreciation. Vera much enjoyed Gallic appreciation. It ravished her to think that she was the light of poor Felix's existence, an unattainable star for him. Of course, Stephen didn't mind. That is to say, he didn't really mind.

The car rushed off in the direction of Exeter, homewards.

That day, by means of Felix's expert illegal driving, they got as far as Bath; and there were no breakdowns. The domestic atmosphere in the tonneau was slightly disturbed at the beginning of the run, but it soon improved. Indeed, after lunch Stephen grew positively bright and gay. At tea, which they took just outside Bristol, he actually went so far as to praise the hat. He said that it was a very becoming hat, and also that it was well worth the money. In a word, he signified to Vera that their first battle had been fought and that Vera had won, and that he meant to make the best of it and accept the situation.

Vera was naturally charmed, and when she was charmed she was charming. She said to herself that she had always known that she could manage a man. The recipe for managing a man was firmness coupled with charm. But there must be no half measures, no hesitations. She had conquered. She saw her future life stretching out before her like a beautiful vista. And Stephen was to be her slave, and she would have nothing to do but to give rein to her caprices, and charm Stephen when he happened to deserve it.

But the next morning the hat had vanished out of the bedroom of the exclusive hotel at Bath. Vera could not believe that it had vanished; but it had. It was not in the hat-box, nor on the couch, nor under the couch, nor perched on a knob of the bedstead, nor in any of the spots where it ought to have been. When she realized that as a fact it had vanished she was cross, and on inquiring from Stephen what trick he had played with her hat, she succeeded in conveying to Stephen that she was cross. Stephen was still in bed, comatose. The tone of his reply startled her.

'Look here, child,' he said, or rather snapped—he had never been snappish before—'since you took the confounded thing off last evening I haven't seen it and I haven't touched it, and I don't know where it is.'

'But you must—'

'I gave in to you about the hat,' Stephen continued to snap, 'though I knew I was a fool to do so, and I consider I behaved pretty pleasantly over it too. But I don't want any more scenes. If you've lost it, that's not my fault.'

Such speeches took Vera very much aback. And she, too, in her turn, now saw the dangers of a quarrel, and in this second altercation it was Stephen who won. He said he would not even mention the disappearance of the hat to the hotel manager. He was sure it must be in one of Vera's trunks. And in the end Vera performed that day's trip in another hat.

They reached the Five Towns much earlier than they had anticipated—before lunch on the ninth day, whereas the new servants in their new house at Bursley were only expecting them for dinner. So Stephen had the agreeable idea of stopping the car in front of the new Hotel Metropole at Hanbridge and lunching there. Precisely opposite this new and luxurious caravanserai (as they love to call it in the Five Towns) is the imposing garage and agency where Stephen had hired the Napier car. Felix said he would lunch hurriedly in order to transact certain business at the garage before taking them on to Bursley. After lunch, however, Vera caught him transacting business with a chambermaid in a corridor. Shocking though the revelation is, it needs to be said that Felix was kissing the chambermaid. The blow to Mrs Cheswardine was severe. She had imagined that Felix spent all his time in gazing up to her as an unattainable star.

She spoke to Stephen about it, in the accents of disillusion. 'What?' cried Stephen. 'Don't you know? They're engaged to be married. Her name is Mary Callear. She used to be parlourmaid at Uncle John's at Oldcastle. But hotels pay higher wages.'

Felix engaged to a parlourmaid! Felix, who had always seemed to Vera a gentleman in disguise! Yes, it was indeed a blow!

But balm awaited Vera at her new home in Bursley. A parcel, obviously containing a cardboard box, had arrived for Stephen. He opened it, and the lost hat was inside it. Stephen read a note, and explained that the hotel people at Bath had found it and forwarded it. He began to praise the hat anew. He made Vera put it on instantly, and seemed delighted. So much so that Vera went out to the porch to say good-bye to Felix in a most forgiving frame of mind. She forgave Felix for being engaged to the chambermaid.

And there was the chambermaid walking up the drive, quite calmly! Felix, also quite calmly, asked Vera to excuse him, and told the chambermaid to get into the car and sit beside him. He then informed Vera that he had to go with the car immediately to Oldcastle, and was taking Miss Callear with him for the run, this being Miss Callear's weekly afternoon off. Miss Callear had come to Bursley in the electric tram.

Vera shook with swift anger; not at Felix's information, but the patent fact that Mary Callear was wearing a hat which was the exact replica of the hat on Vera's own head. And Mary Callear was seated like a duchess in the car, while Vera stood on the gravel. And two of Vera's new servants were there to see that Vera was wearing a hat precisely equivalent to the hat of a chambermaid!

She went abruptly into the house and sought for Stephen—as with a sword. But Stephen was not discoverable. She ran to her elegant new bedroom and shut herself in. She understood the plot. She had plenty of wit. Stephen had concerted it with Felix. In spite of Stephen's allegations of innocence, the hat had been sent somewhere—probably to Brunt's at Hanbridge—to be copied at express speed, and Stephen had presented the copy to Felix, in order that Felix might present it to Mary Callear the chambermaid, and the meeting in the front garden had been deliberately arranged by that odious male, Stephen. Truly, she had not believed Stephen capable of such duplicity and cruelty.

She removed the hat, gazed at it, and then tore it to pieces and scattered the pieces on the carpet.

An hour later Stephen crept into the bedroom and beheld the fragments, and smiled.

'Stephen,' she exclaimed, 'you're a horrid, cruel brute.' 'I know I am,' said Stephen. 'You ought to have found that out long since.'

'I won't love you any more. It's all over,' she sobbed. But he just kissed her.

VERA'S FIRST CHRISTMAS ADVENTURE

I

Five days before Christmas, Cheswardine came home to his wife from a week's sojourn in London on business. Vera, in her quality of the best-dressed woman in Bursley, met him on the doorstep (or thereabouts) of their charming but childless home, attired in a teagown that would have ravished a far less impressionable male than her husband; while he, in his quality of a prosaic and flourishing earthenware manufacturer, pretended to take the teagown as a matter of course, and gave her the sober, solid kiss of a man who has been married six years and is getting used to it.

Still, the teagown had pleased him, and by certain secret symptoms Vera knew that it had pleased him. She hoped much from that teagown. She hoped that he had come home in a more pacific temper than he had shown when he left her, and that she would carry her point after all.

Now, naturally, when a husband in easy circumstances, the possessor of a pretty and pampered wife, spends a week in London and returns five days before Christmas, certain things are rightly and properly to be expected from him. It would need an astounding courage, an amazing lack of a sense of the amenity of conjugal existence in such a husband to enable him to disappoint such reasonable expectations. And Cheswardine, though capable of pulling the curb very tight on the caprices of his wife, was a highly decent fellow. He had no intention to disappoint; he knew his duty.

So that during afternoon tea with the teagown in a cosy corner of the great Chippendale drawing-room he began to unfasten a small wooden case which he had brought into the house in his own hand, opened it with considerable precaution, making a fine mess of packing-stuff on the carpet, and gradually drew to light a pair of vases of Venetian glass. He put them on the mantlepiece.

'There!' he said, proudly, and with a virtuous air.

They were obviously costly antique vases, exquisite in form, exquisite in the graduated tints of their pale blue and rose.

'Seventeenth century!' he said.

'They're very nice,' Vera agreed, with a show of enthusiasm. What are they for?'

'Your Christmas present,' Cheswardine explained, and added 'my dear!'

'Oh, Stephen!' she murmured.

A kiss on these occasions is only just, and Cheswardine had one.

'Duveens told me they were quite unique,' he said, modestly; 'and I believe 'em.'

You might imagine that a pair of Venetian vases of the seventeenth century, stated by Duveens to be unique, would have satisfied a woman who had a generous dress allowance and lacked absolutely nothing that was essential. But Vera was not satisfied. She was, on the contrary, profoundly disappointed. For the presence of those vases proved that she had not carried her point. They deprived her of hope. The unpleasantness before Cheswardine went to London had been more or less a propos of a Christmas present. Vera had seen in Bostock's vast emporium in the neighbouring town of Hanbridge, a music-stool in the style known as art nouveau, which had enslaved her fancy. She had taken her husband to see it, and it had not enslaved her husband's fancy in the slightest degree. It was made in light woods, and the woods were curved and twisted as though they had recently spent seven years in a purgatory for sinful trees. Here and there in the design onyx- stones had been set in the wood. The seat itself was beautifully soft. What captured Vera was chiefly the fact that it did not open at the top, as most elaborate music-stools do, but at either side. You pressed a button (onyx) and the panel fell down displaying your music in little compartments ready to hand; and the eastern moiety of the music-stool was for piano pieces, and the western moiety for songs. In short, it was the last word of music-stools; nothing could possibly be newer.

But Cheswardine did not like it, and did not conceal his opinion. He argued that it would not 'go' with the Chippendale furniture, and Vera said that all beautiful things 'went' together, and Cheswardine admitted that they did, rather dryly. You see, they took the matter seriously because the house was their hobby; they were always changing its interior, which was more than they could have done for a child, even if they had had one; and Cheswardine's finer and soberer taste was always fighting against Vera's predilection for the novel and the bizarre. Apart from clothes, Vera had not much more than the taste of a mouse.

They did not quarrel in Bostock's. Indeed, they did not quarrel anywhere; but after Vera had suggested that he might at any rate humour her by giving her the music-stool for a Christmas present (she seemed to think this would somehow help it to 'go' with the Chippendale), and Cheswardine had politely but firmly declined, there had been a certain coolness and quite six tears. Vera had caused it to be understood that even if Cheswardine was NOT interested in music, even if he did hate music and did call the Broadwood ebony grand ugly, that was no reason why she should be deprived of a pretty and original music-stool that would keep her music tidy and that would be HERS. As for it not going with the Chippendale, that was simply an excuse ... etc.

Hence it is not surprising that the Venetian vases of the seventeenth century left Vera cold, and that the domestic prospects for Christmas were a little cold.

However, Vera, with wifely and submissive tact made the best of things; and that evening she began to decorate the hall, dining- room, and drawing-room with holly and mistletoe. Before the pair retired to rest, the true Christmas feeling, slightly tinged with a tender melancholy, permeated the house, and the servants were growing excited in advance. The servants weren't going to have a dinner-party, with crackers and port and a table-centre unmatched in the Five Towns; the servants weren't going to invite their friends to an evening's jollity. The servants were merely going to work somewhat harder and have somewhat less sleep; but such is the magical effect of holly and mistletoe twined round picture-cords and hung under chandeliers that the excitement of the servants was entirely pleasurable.

And as Vera shut the bedroom door, she said, with a delightful, forgiving smile—

'I saw a lovely cigar-cabinet at Bostock's yesterday.'

'Oh!' said Cheswardine, touched. He had no cigar-cabinet, and he wanted one, and Vera knew that he wanted one.

And Vera slept in the sweet consciousness of her thoughtful wifeliness.

The next morning, at breakfast, Cheswardine demanded—

'Getting pretty hard up, aren't you, Maria?'

He called her Maria when he wished to be arch.

Well,' she said, 'as a matter of fact, I am. What with the—'

And he gave her a five-pound note.

It happened so every year. He provided her with the money to buy him a Christmas present. But it is, I hope, unnecessary to say that the connection between her present to him and the money he furnished was never crudely mentioned.

She made an opportunity, before he left for the works, to praise the Venetian vases, and she insisted that he should wrap up well, because he was showing signs of one of his bad colds.

II

In the early afternoon she went to Bostock's emporium, at Hanbridge, to buy the cigar-cabinet and a few domestic trifles. Bostock's is a good shop. I do not say that it has the classic and serene dignity of Brunt's, over the way, where one orders one's dining-room suites and one's frocks for the January dances. But it is a good shop, and one of the chief glories of the Paris of the Five Towns. It has frontages in three streets, and it might be called the shop of the hundred windows. You can buy pretty nearly anything at Bostock's, from an art nouveau music-stool up to the highest cheese—for there is a provision department. (You can't get cheese at Brunt's.)

Vera made her uninteresting purchases first, in the basement, and then she went up-stairs to the special Christmas department, which certainly was wonderful: a blaze and splendour of electric light; a glitter of gilded iridescent toys and knick-knacks; a smiling, excited, pushing multitude of faces, young and old; and the cashiers in their cages gathering in money as fast as they could lay their tired hands on it! A joyous, brilliant scene, calculated to bring soft tears of satisfaction to the board of directors that presided over Bostock's. It was a record Christmas for Bostock's. The electric cars were thundering over the frozen streets of all the Five Towns to bring customers to Bostock's. Children dreamt of Bostock's. Fathers went to scoff and remained to pay. Brunt's was not exactly alarmed, for nothing could alarm Brunt's; but there was just a sort of suspicion of something in the air at Brunt's that did not make for odious self-conceit. People seemed to become intoxicated when they went into Bostock's, to close their heads in a frenzy of buying.

And there the art nouveau music-stool stood in the corner, where Vera had originally seen it! She approached it, not thinking of the terrible danger. The compartments for music lay invitingly open.

'Four pounds, nine and six, Mrs Cheswardine,' said a shop-walker, who knew her.

She stopped to finger it.

Well, of course everybody is acquainted with that peculiar ecstasy that undoubtedly does overtake you in good shops, sometimes, especially at Christmas. I prefer to call it ecstasy rather than intoxication, but I have heard it called even drunkenness. It is a magnificent and overwhelming experience, like a good wine. A blind instinct seizes your reason and throws her out of the window of your soul, and then assumes entire control of the volitional machinery. You listen to no arguments, you care for no consequences. You want a thing; you must have it; you do have it.

Vera was caught unawares by this magnificent and overwhelming experience, just as she stooped to finger the music-stool. A fig for the cigar-cabinet! A fig for her husband's objections! After all she was a grown-up woman (twenty-nine or thirty), and entitled to a certain freedom. She was not and would not be a slave. It would look perfect in the drawing-room.

'I'll take it,' she said.

'Yes, Mrs Cheswardine. A unique thing, quite unique. Penkethman!'

And Vera followed Penkethman to a cash desk and received half-a- guinea out of a five-pound note.

'I want it carefully packed,' said Vera.

'Yes, ma'am. It will be delivered in the morning.'

She was just beginning to realize that she had been under the sinister influence of the ecstasy, and that she had not bought the cigar-cabinet, and that she had practically no more money, and that Stephen's rule against credit was the strictest of all his rules, when she caught sight of Mr Charles Woodruff buying toys, doubtless for his nephews and nieces.

Mr Woodruff was the bachelor friend of the family. He had loved Vera before Stephen loved her, and he was still attached to her. Stephen and he were chums of the most advanced kind. Why! Stephen and Vera thought nothing of bickering in front of Mr Woodruff, who rated them both and sided with neither.

'Hello!' said Woodruff, flushing, and moving his long, clumsy limbs when she touched him on the shoulder. 'I'm just buying a few toys.'

She helped him to buy toys, and then he asked her to go and have tea with him at the newly-opened Sub Rosa Tea Rooms, in Machin Street. She agreed, and, in passing the music-stool, gave a small parcel which she was carrying to Penkethman, and told him he might as well put it in the music-stool. She was glad to have tea with Charlie Woodruff. It would distract her, prevent her from thinking. The ecstasy had almost died out, and she had a violent desire not to think.

III

A terrible blow fell upon her the next morning. Stephen had one of his bad colds, one of his worst. The mere cold she could have supported with fortitude, but he was forced to remain indoors, and his presence in the house she could not support with fortitude. The music-stool would be sure to arrive before lunch, and he would be there to see it arrive. The ecstasy had fully expired now, and she had more leisure to think than she wanted. She could not imagine what mad instinct had compelled her to buy the music- stool. (Once out of the shop these instincts always are difficult to imagine.) She knew that Stephen would be angry. He might perhaps go to the length of returning the music-stool whence it came. For, though she was a pretty and pampered woman, Stephen had a way, in the last resort, of being master of his own house. And she could not even placate him with the gift of a cigar-cabinet. She could not buy a five-guinea cigar-cabinet with ten and six. She had no other money in the world. She never had money, yet money was always running through her fingers. Stephen treated her generously, gave her an ample allowance, but he would under no circumstances permit credit, nor would he pay her allowance in advance. She had nothing to expect till the New Year.

She attended to his cold, and telephoned to the works for a clerk to come up, and she refrained from telling Stephen that he must have been very careless while in London, to catch a cold like that. Her self-denial in this respect surprised Stephen, but he put it down to the beneficent influence of Christmas and the Venetian vases.

Bostock's pair-horse van arrived before the garden gate earlier than her worse fears had anticipated, and Bostock's men were evidently in a tremendous hurry that morning. In quite an abnormally small number of seconds the wooden case containing the fragile music-stool was lying in the inner hall, waiting to be unpacked. Having signed the delivery-book Vera stood staring at the accusatory package. Stephen was lounging over the dining-room fire, perhaps dozing. She would have the thing swiftly transported up-stairs and hidden in an attic for a time.

But just then Stephen popped out of the dining-room. Stephen's masculine curiosity had been aroused by the advent of Bostock's van. He had observed the incoming of the package from the window, and he had ventured to the hall to inspect it. The event had roused him wonderfully from the heavy torpor which a cold induces. He wore a dressing-gown, the pockets of which bulged with handkerchiefs.

'You oughtn't to be out here, Stephen,' said his wife.

'Nonsense!' he said. 'Why, upon my soul, this steam heat is warmer than the dining-room fire.' Vera, silenced by the voice of truth, could not reply.

Stephen bent his great height to inspect the package. It was an appetizing Christmas package; straw escaped from between its ribs, and it had an air of being filled with something at once large and delicate.

'Oh!' observed Stephen, humorously. 'Ah! So this is it, is it? Ah! Oh! Very good!'

And he walked round it.

How on earth had he learnt that she had bought it? She had not mentioned the purchase to Mr Woodruff.

'Yes, Stephen,' she said timidly. 'That's it, and I hope—'

'It ought to hold a tidy few cigars, that ought,' remarked Stephen complacently.

He took it for the cigar-cabinet!

She paused, struck. She had to make up her mind in an instant.

'Oh yes,' she murmured.

'A thousand?'

'Yes, a thousand,' she said.

'I thought so,' murmured Stephen. 'I mustn't kiss you, because I've got a cold,' said he. 'But, all the same I'm awfully obliged, Vera. Suppose we have it opened now, eh? Then we could decide where it is to go, and I could put my cigars in it.'

'Oh no,' she protested. 'Oh no, Stephen! That's not fair! It mustn't be opened before Christmas morning.'

'But I gave you my vases yesterday.'

'That's different,' she said. 'Christmas is Christmas.' 'Oh, very well,' he yielded. 'That's all right, my dear.'

Then he began to sniff.

'There's a deuced odd smell from it,' he said.

'Perhaps it's the wood!' she faltered.

'I hope it isn't,' he said. 'I expect it's the straw. A deuced odd smell. We'll have the thing put in the side hall, next to the clock. It will be out of the way there. And I can come and gaze at it when I feel depressed. Eh, Maria?' He was undoubtedly charmed at the prospect of owning so large and precious a cigar-cabinet.

Considering that the parcel which she had given to Penkethman to put in the music-stool comprised a half-a-pound of Bostock's very ripest Gorgonzola cheese, bought at the cook's special request, the smell which proceeded from the mysterious inwards of the packing-case did not surprise Vera at all. But it disconcerted her none the less. And she wondered how she could get the cheese out.

For thirty hours the smell from the unopened packing-case waxed in vigour and strength. Stephen's cold grew worse and prevented him from appreciating its full beauty, but he savoured enough of it to induce him to compare it facetiously to the effluvium of a dead rat, and he said several times that Bostock's really ought to use better straw. He was frequently to be seen in the hall, gloating over his cigar-cabinet. Once he urged Vera to have it opened and so get rid of the straw, but she refused, and found the nerve to tell him that he was exaggerating the odour.

She was at a loss what to do. She could not get up in the middle of the night and unpack the package and hide its guilty secret. Indeed, to unpack the package would bring about her ruin instantly; for, the package unpacked, Stephen would naturally expect to see the cigar-cabinet. And so the hours crept on to Christmas and Vera's undoing. She gave herself a headache.

It was just thirty hours after the arrival of the package when Mr Woodruff dropped in for tea. Stephen was asleep in the dining- room, which apartment he particularly affected during his colds. Woodruff was shown into the drawing-room, where Vera was having her headache. Vera brightened. In fact, she suddenly grew very bright. And she gave Woodruff tea, and took some herself, and Woodruff passed an enjoyable twenty minutes.

The two Venetian vases were on the mantelpiece. Vera rose into ecstasies about them, and called upon Charlie Woodruff to rise too. He got up from his chair to examine the vases, which Vera had placed close together side by side at the corner of the mantelpiece nearest to him. Vera and Woodruff also stood close together side by side. And just as Woodruff was about to handle the vases, Vera knocked his arm; his arm collided with one vase; that vase collided with the next, and both fell to earth—to the hard, unfeeling, unyielding tiles of the hearth.

IV

They were smashed to atoms.

Vera screamed. She screamed twice, and ran out of the room.

'Stephen, Stephen!' she cried hysterically. 'Charlie has broken my vases, both of them. It IS too bad of him. He's really too clumsy!'

There was a terrific pother. Stephen wakened violently, and in a moment all three were staring ineffectually at the thousand crystal fragments on the hearth.

'But—' began Charlie Woodruff.

And that was all he did say.

He and Vera and Stephen had been friends since infancy, so she had the right not to conceal her feelings before him; Stephen had the same right. They both exercised it.

'But—' began Charlie again.

'Oh, never mind,' Stephen stopped him curtly. 'Accidents can't be helped.'

'I shall get another pair,' said Woodruff.

'No, you won't,' replied Stephen. 'You can't. There isn't another pair in the world. See?'

The two men simultaneously perceived that Vera was weeping. She was very pretty in tears, but that did not prevent the masculine world from feeling awkward and self-conscious. Charlie had notions about going out and burying himself.

'Come, Vera, come,' her husband enjoined, blowing his nose with unnecessary energy, bad as his cold was.

'I—I liked those vases more than anything you've—you've ever given me,' Vera blubbered, charmingly, patting her eyes.

Stephen glanced at Woodruff, as who should say: 'Well, my boy, you uncorked those tears, I'll leave you to deal with 'em. You see, I'm an invalid in a dressing-gown. I leave you.'

And went.

'No-but-look-here-I-say,' Charlie Woodruff expostulated to Vera when he was alone with her—he often started an expostulation with that singular phrase. 'I'm awfully sorry. I don't know how it happened. You must let me give you something else.'

Vera shook her head.

'No,' she said. 'I wanted Stephen awfully to give me that music- stool that I told you about a fortnight ago. But he gave me the vases instead, and I liked them ever so much better.'

'I shall give you the music-stool. If you wanted it a fortnight ago, you want it now. It won't make up for the vases, of course, but—'

'No, no,' said Vera, positively.

'Why not?'

'I do not wish you to give me anything. It wouldn't be quite nice,' Vera insisted.

'But I give you something every Christmas.'

'Do you?' asked Vera, innocently.

'Yes, and you and Stephen give me something.'

'Besides, Stephen doesn't quite like the music-stool.'

'What's that got to do with it? You like it. I'm giving it to you, not to him. I shall go over to Bostock's tomorrow morning and get it.'

'I forbid you to.'

'I shall.'

Woodruff departed.

Within five minutes the Cheswardine coachman was driving off in the dogcart to Hanbridge, with the packing-case in the back of the cart, and a note. He brought back the cigar-cabinet. Stephen had not stirred from the dining-room, afraid to encounter a tearful wife. Presently his wife came into the dining-room bearing the vast load of the cigar-cabinet in her delicate arms.

'I thought it might amuse you to fill it with your cigars—just to pass the time,' she said.

Stephen's thought was: 'Well, women take the cake.' It was a thought that occurs frequently to the husbands of Veras.

There was ripe Gorgonzola at dinner. Stephen met it as one meets a person whom one fancies one has met somewhere but cannot remember where.

The next afternoon the music-stool came, for the second time, into the house. Charlie brought it in HIS dogcart. It was unpacked ostentatiously by the radiant Vera. What could Stephen say in depreciation of this gift from their oldest and best friend? As a fact he could and did say a great deal. But he said it when he happened to be all alone in the drawing-room, and had observed the appalling way in which the music-stool did not 'go' with the Chippendale.

'Look at the d—thing!' he exclaimed to himself. 'Look at it!'

However, the Christmas dinner-party was a brilliant success, and after it Vera sat on the art nouveau music-stool and twittered songs, and what with her being so attractive and birdlike, and what with the Christmas feeling in the air... well, Stephen resigned himself to the music-stool.

THE MURDER OF THE MANDARIN

I

'What's that you're saying about murder?' asked Mrs Cheswardine as she came into the large drawing-room, carrying the supper-tray.

'Put it down here,' said her husband, referring to the supper- tray, and pointing to a little table which stood two legs off and two legs on the hearth-rug.

'That apron suits you immensely,' murmured Woodruff, the friend of the family, as he stretched his long limbs into the fender towards the fire, farther even than the long limbs of Cheswardine. Each man occupied an easy-chair on either side of the hearth; each was very tall, and each was forty.

Mrs Cheswardine, with a whisk infinitely graceful, set the tray on the table, took a seat behind it on a chair that looked like a toddling grand-nephew of the arm-chairs, and nervously smoothed out the apron.

As a matter of fact, the apron did suit her immensely. It is astounding, delicious, adorable, the effect of a natty little domestic apron suddenly put on over an elaborate and costly frock, especially when you can hear the rustle of a silk petticoat beneath, and more especially when the apron is smoothed out by jewelled fingers. Every man knows this. Every woman knows it. Mrs Cheswardine knew it. In such matters Mrs Cheswardine knew exactly what she was about. She delighted, when her husband brought Woodruff in late of a night, as he frequently did after a turn at the club, to prepare with her own hands—the servants being in bed—a little snack of supper for them. Tomato sandwiches, for instance, miraculously thin, together with champagne or Bass. The men preferred Bass, naturally, but if Mrs Cheswardine had a fancy for a sip of champagne out of her husband's tumbler, Bass was not forthcoming.

Tonight it was champagne.

Woodruff opened it, as he always did, and involuntarily poured out a libation on the hearth, as he almost always did. Good-natured, ungainly, long-suffering men seldom achieve the art of opening champagne.

Mrs Cheswardine tapped her pink-slippered foot impatiently.

'You're all nerves tonight,' Woodruff laughed, 'and you've made me nervous,' And at length he got some of the champagne into a tumbler.

'No, I'm not,' Mrs Cheswardine contradicted him.

'Yes, you are, Vera,' Woodruff insisted calmly.

She smiled. The use of that elegant Christian name, with its faint suggestion of Russian archduchesses, had a strange effect on her, particularly from the lips of Woodruff. She was proud of it, and of her surname too—one of the oldest surnames in the Five Towns. The syllables of 'Vera' invariably soothed her, like a charm. Woodruff, and Cheswardine also, had called her Vera during the whole of her life; and she was thirty. They had all three lived in different houses at the top end of Trafalgar Road, Bursley. Woodruff fell in love with her first, when she was eighteen, but with no practical result. He was a brown-haired man, personable despite his ungainliness, but he failed to perceive that to worship from afar off is not the best way to capture a young woman with large eyes and an emotional disposition. Cheswardine, who had a black beard, simply came along and married the little thing. She fluttered down on to his shoulders like a pigeon. She adored him, feared him, cooed to him, worried him, and knew that there were depths of his mind which she would never plumb. Woodruff, after being best man, went on loving, meekly and yet philosophically, and found his chief joy in just these suppers. The arrangement suited Vera; and as for the husband and the hopeless admirer, they had always been fast friends.

'I asked you what you were saying about murder,' said Vera sharply, 'but it seems—'

'Oh! did you?' Woodruff apologized. 'I was saying that murder isn't such an impossible thing as it appears. Anyone might commit a murder.'

'Then you want to defend, Harrisford? Do you hear what he says, Stephen?'

The notorious and terrible Harrisford murders were agitating the Five Towns that November. People read, talked, and dreamt murder; for several weeks they took murder to all their meals.

'He doesn't want to defend Harrisford at all,' said Cheswardine, with a superior masculine air, 'and of course anyone might commit a murder. I might.'

'Stephen! How horrid you are!' 'You might, even!' said Woodruff, gazing at Vera.

'Charlie! Why, the blood alone—'

'There isn't always blood,' said the oracular husband.

'Listen here,' proceeded Woodruff, who read variously and enjoyed philosophical speculation. 'Supposing that by just taking thought, by just wishing it, an Englishman could kill a mandarin in China and make himself rich for life, without anybody knowing anything about it! How many mandarins do you suppose there would be left in China at the end of a week!'

'At the end of twenty-four hours, rather,' said Cheswardine grimly.

'Not one,' said Woodruff.

'But that's absurd,' Vera objected, disturbed. When these two men began their philosophical discussions they always succeeded in disturbing her. She hated to see life in a queer light. She hated to think.

'It isn't absurd,' Woodruff replied. 'It simply shows that what prevents wholesale murder is not the wickedness of it, but the fear of being found out, and the general mess, and seeing the corpse, and so on.'

Vera shuddered.

'And I'm not sure,' Woodruff proceeded, 'that murder is so very much more wicked than lots of other things.'

'Usury, for instance,' Cheswardine put in.

'Or bigamy,' said Woodruff.

'But an Englishman COULDN'T kill a mandarin in China by just wishing it,' said Vera, looking up.

'How do we know?' said Woodruff, in his patient voice. 'How do we know? You remember what I was telling you about thought- transference last week. It was in Borderland.'

Vera felt as if there was no more solid ground to stand on, and it angered her to be plunging about in a bog.

'I think it's simply silly,' she remarked. 'No, thanks.'

She said 'No, thanks' to her husband, when he tendered his glass.

He moved the glass still closer to her lips.

'I said "No, thanks,"' she repeated dryly.

'Just a mouthful,' he urged.

'I'm not thirsty.'

'Then you'd better go to bed,' said he.

He had a habit of sending her to bed abruptly. She did not dislike it. But she had various ways of going. Tonight it was the way of an archduchess.

II

Woodruff, in stating that Vera was all nerves that evening, was quite right. She was. And neither her husband nor Woodruff knew the reason.

The reason had to do most intimately with frocks.

Vera had been married ten years. But no one would have guessed it, to watch her girlish figure and her birdlike ways. You see, she was the only child in the house. She often bitterly regretted the absence of offspring to the name and honour of Cheswardine. She envied other wives their babies. She doted on babies. She said continually that in her deliberate opinion the proper mission of women was babies. She was the sort of woman that regards a cathedral as a place built especially to sit in and dream soft domestic dreams; the sort of woman that adores music simply because it makes her dream. And Vera's brown studies, which were frequent, consisted chiefly of babies. But as babies amused themselves by coming down the chimneys of all the other houses in Bursley, and avoiding her house, she sought comfort in frocks. She made the best of herself. And it was a good best. Her figure was as near perfect as a woman's can be, and then there were those fine emotional eyes, and that flutteringness of the pigeon, and an ever-changing charm of gesture. Vera had become the best-dressed woman in Bursley. And that is saying something. Her husband was wealthy, with an increasing income, though, of course, as an earthenware manufacturer, and the son and grandson of an earthenware manufacturer, he joined heartily in the general Five Towns lamentation that there was no longer any money to be made out of 'pots'. He liked to have a well-dressed woman about the house, and he allowed her an incredible allowance, the amount of which was breathed with awe among Vera's friends; a hundred a year, in fact. He paid it to her quarterly, by cheque. Such was his method.

Now a ball was to be given by the members of the Ladies' Hockey Club (or such of them as had not been maimed for life in the pursuit of this noble pastime) on the very night after the conversation about murder. Vera belonged to the Hockey Club (in a purely ornamental sense), and she had procured a frock for the ball which was calculated to crown her reputation as a mirror of elegance. The skirt had—but no (see the columns of the Staffordshire Signal for the 9th November, 1901). The mischief was that the gown lacked, for its final perfection, one particular thing, and that particular thing was separated from Vera by the glass front of Brunt's celebrated shop at Hanbridge. Vera could have managed without it. The gown would still have been brilliant without it. But Vera had seen it, and she WANTED it.

Its cost was a guinea. Well, you will say, what is a guinea to a dainty creature with a hundred a year? Let her go and buy the article. The point is that she couldn't, because she had only six and sevenpence left in the wide world. (And six weeks to Christmas!) She had squandered—oh, soul above money!—twenty-five pounds, and more than twenty-five pounds, since the 29th of September. Well, you will say, credit, in other words, tick? No, no, no! The giant Stephen absolutely and utterly forbade her to procure anything whatever on credit. She was afraid of him. She knew just how far she could go with Stephen. He was great and terrible. Well, you will say, why couldn't she blandish and cajole Stephen for a sovereign or so? Impossible! She had a hundred a year on the clear understanding that it was never exceeded nor anticipated. Well, you will discreetly hint, there are certain devices known to housewives.... Hush! Vera had already employed them. Six and sevenpence was not merely all that remained to her of her dress allowance; it was all that remained to her of her household allowance till the next Monday.

Hence her nerves.

There that poor unfortunate woman lay, with her unconscious tyrant of a husband snoring beside her, desolately wakeful under the night-light in the large, luxurious bedroom—three servants sleeping overhead, champagne in the cellar, furs in the wardrobe, valuable lace round her neck at that very instant, grand piano in the drawing-room, horses in the stable, stuffed bear in the hall— and her life was made a blank for want of fourteen and fivepence! And she had nobody to confide in. How true it is that the human soul is solitary, that content is the only true riches, and that to be happy we must be good!

It was at that juncture of despair that she thought of mandarins. Or rather—I may as well be frank—she had been thinking of mandarins all the time since retiring to rest. There MIGHT be something in Charlie's mandarin theory.... According to Charlie, so many queer, inexplicable things happened in the world. Occult— subliminal—astral—thoughtwaves. These expressions and many more occurred to her as she recollected Charlie's disconcerting conversations. There MIGHT.... One never knew.

Suddenly she thought of her husband's pockets, bulging with silver, with gold, and with bank-notes. Tantalizing vision! No! She could not steal. Besides, he might wake up.

And she returned to mandarins. She got herself into a very morbid and two-o'clock-in-the-morning state of mind. Suppose it was a dodge that DID work. (Of course, she was extremely superstitious; we all are.) She began to reflect seriously upon China. She remembered having heard that Chinese mandarins were very corrupt; that they ground the faces of the poor, and put innocent victims to the torture; in short, that they were sinful and horrid persons, scoundrels unfit for mercy. Then she pondered upon the remotest parts of China, regions where Europeans never could penetrate. No doubt there was some unimportant mandarin, somewhere in these regions, to whose district his death would be a decided blessing, to kill whom would indeed be an act of humanity. Probably a mandarin without wife or family; a bachelor mandarin whom no relative would regret; or, in the alternative, a mandarin with many wives, whose disgusting polygamy merited severe punishment! An old mandarin already pretty nearly dead; or, in the alternative, a young one just commencing a career of infamy!

'I'm awfully silly,' she whispered to herself. 'But still, if there SHOULD be anything in it. And I must, I must, I must have that thing for my dress!'

She looked again at the dim forms of her husband's clothes, pitched anyhow on an ottoman. No! She could not stoop to theft!

So she murdered a mandarin; lying in bed there; not any particular mandarin, a vague mandarin, the mandarin most convenient and suitable under all the circumstances. She deliberately wished him dead, on the off-chance of acquiring riches, or, more accurately, because she was short of fourteen and fivepence in order to look perfectly splendid at a ball.

In the morning when she woke up—her husband had already departed to the works—she thought how foolish she had been in the night. She did not feel sorry for having desired the death of a fellow- creature. Not at all. She felt sorry because she was convinced, in the cold light of day, that the charm would not work. Charlie's notions were really too ridiculous, too preposterous. No! She must reconcile herself to wearing a ball dress which was less than perfection, and all for the want of fourteen and fivepence. And she had more nerves than ever!

She had nerves to such an extent that when she went to unlock the drawer of her own private toilet-table, in which her prudent and fussy husband forced her to lock up her rings and brooches every night, she attacked the wrong drawer—an empty unfastened drawer that she never used. And lo! the empty drawer was not empty. There was a sovereign lying in it!

This gave her a start, connecting the discovery, as naturally at the first blush she did, with the mandarin.

Surely it couldn't be, after all.

Then she came to her senses. What absurdity! A coincidence, of course, nothing else? Besides, a mere sovereign! It wasn't enough. Charlie had said 'rich for life'. The sovereign must have lain there for months and months, forgotten.

However, it was none the less a sovereign. She picked it up, thanked Providence, ordered the dog-cart, and drove straight to Brunt's. The particular thing that she acquired was an exceedingly thin, slim, and fetching silver belt—a marvel for the money, and the ideal waist decoration for her wonderful white muslin gown. She bought it, and left the shop.

And as she came out of the shop, she saw a street urchin holding out the poster of the early edition of the Signal. And she read on the poster, in large letters: 'DEATH OF LI HUNG CHANG.' It is no exaggeration to say that she nearly fainted. Only by the exercise of that hard self-control, of which women alone are capable, did she refrain from tumbling against the blue-clad breast of Adams, the Cheswardine coachman.

She purchased the Signal with well-feigned calm, opened it and read: 'Stop-press news. Pekin. Li Hung Chang, the celebrated Chinese statesman, died at two o'clock this morning.—Reuter.'

III

Vera reclined on the sofa that afternoon, and the sofa was drawn round in front of the drawing-room fire. And she wore her fluffiest and languidest peignoir. And there was a perfume of eau de Cologne in the apartment. Vera was having a headache; she was having it in her grand, her official manner. Stephen had had to lunch alone. He had been told that in all probability his suffering wife would not be well enough to go to the ball. Whereupon he had grunted. As a fact, Vera's headache was extremely real, and she was very upset indeed.

The death of Li Hung Chang was heavy on her soul. Occultism was justified of itself. The affair lay beyond coincidence. She had always KNOWN that there was something in occultism, supernaturalism, so-called superstitions, what not. But she had never expected to prove the faith that was in her by such a homicidal act on her own part. It was detestable of Charlie to have mentioned the thing at all. He had no right to play with fire. And as for her husband, words could give but the merest rough outline of her resentment against Stephen. A pretty state of things that a woman with a position such as she had to keep up should be reduced to six and sevenpence! Stephen, no doubt, expected her to visit the pawnshop. It would serve him right if she did so—and he met her coming out under the three brass balls! Did she not dress solely and wholly to please him? Not in the least to please herself! Personally she had a mind set on higher things, impossible aspirations. But he liked fine clothes. And it was her duty to satisfy him. She strove to satisfy him in all matters. She lived for him. She sacrificed herself to him completely. And what did she get in return? Nothing! Nothing! Nothing! All men were selfish. And women were their victims.... Stephen, with his silly bullying rules against credit and so forth.... The worst of men was that they had no sense.

She put a new dose of eau de Cologne on her forehead, and leaned on one elbow. On the mantelpiece lay the tissue parcel containing the slim silver belt, the price of Li's death. She wanted to stick it in the fire. And only the fact that it would not burn prevented her savagely doing so. There was something wrong, too, with the occultism. To receive a paltry sovereign for murdering the greatest statesman of the Eastern hemisphere was simply grotesque. Moreover, she had most distinctly not wanted to deprive China of a distinguished man. She had expressly stipulated for an inferior and insignificant mandarin, one that could be spared and that was unknown to Reuter. She supposed she ought to have looked up China at the Wedgwood Institution and selected a definite mandarin with a definite place of residence. But could she be expected to go about a murder deliberately like that?

With regard to the gross inadequacy of the fiscal return for her deed, perhaps that was her own fault. She had not wished for more. Her brain had been so occupied by the belt that she had wished only for the belt. But, perhaps, on the other hand, vast wealth was to come. Perhaps something might occur that very night. That would be better. Yet would it be better? However rich she might become, Stephen would coolly take charge of her riches, and dole them out to her, and make rules for her concerning them. And besides, Charlie would suspect her guilt. Charlie understood her, and perused her thoughts far better than Stephen did. She would never be able to conceal the truth from Charlie. The conversation, the death of Li within two hours, and then a sudden fortune accruing to her—Charlie would inevitably put two and two together and divine her shameful secret.

The outlook was thoroughly black anyway.

She then fell asleep.

When she awoke, some considerable time afterwards, Stephen was calling to her. It was his voice, indeed, that had aroused her. The room was dark.

'I say, Vera,' he demanded, in a low, slightly inimical tone, 'have you taken a sovereign out of the empty drawer in your toilet-table?'

'No,' she said quickly, without thinking.

'Ah!' he observed reflectively, 'I knew I was right.' He paused, and added, coldly, 'If you aren't better you ought to go to bed.'

Then he left her, shutting the door with a noise that showed a certain lack of sympathy with her headache.

She sprang up. Her first feeling was one of thankfulness that that brief interview had occurred in darkness. So Stephen was aware of the existence of the sovereign! The sovereign was not occult. Possibly he had put it there. And what did he know he was 'right' about?

She lighted the gas, and gazed at herself in the glass, realizing that she no longer had a headache, and endeavouring to arrange her ideas.

'What's this?' said another voice at the door. She glanced round hastily, guiltily. It was Charlie.

'Steve telephoned me you were too ill to go to the dance,' explained Charlie, 'so I thought I'd come and make inquiries. I quite expected to find you in bed with a nurse and a doctor or two at least. What is it?' He smiled.

'Nothing,' she replied. 'Only a headache. It's gone now.'

She stood against the mantelpiece, so that he should not see the white parcel.

'That's good,' said Charlie.

There was a pause.

'Strange, Li Hung Chang dying last night, just after we had been talking about killing mandarins,' she said. She could not keep off the subject. It attracted her like a snake, and she approached it in spite of the fact that she fervently wished not to approach it.

'Yes,' said Charlie. 'But Li wasn't a mandarin, you know. And he didn't die after we had been talking about mandarins. He died before.'

'Oh! I thought it said in the paper he died at two o'clock this morning.'

'Two a.m. in Pekin,' Charlie answered. 'You must remember that Pekin time is many hours earlier than our time. It lies so far eastward.'

'Oh!' she said again.

Stephen hurried in, with a worried air.

'Ah! It's you, Charlie!'

'She isn't absolutely dying, I find,' said Charlie, turning to Vera: 'You are going to the dance after all—aren't you?'

'I say, Vera,' Stephen interrupted, 'either you or I must have a scene with Martha. I've always suspected that confounded housemaid. So I put a marked sovereign in a drawer this morning, and it was gone at lunch-time. She'd better hook it instantly. Of course I shan't prosecute.'

'Martha!' cried Vera. 'Stephen, what on earth are you thinking of? I wish you would leave the servants to me. If you think you can manage this house in your spare time from the works, you are welcome to try. But don't blame me for the consequences.' Glances of triumph flashed in her eyes.

'But I tell you—'

'Nonsense,' said Vera. 'I took the sovereign. I saw it there and I took it, and just to punish you, I've spent it. It's not at all nice to lay traps for servants like that.'

'Then why did you tell me just now you hadn't taken it?' Stephen demanded crossly.

'I didn't feel well enough to argue with you then,' Vera replied.

'You've recovered precious quick,' retorted Stephen with grimness.

'Of course, if you want to make a scene before strangers,' Vera whimpered (poor Charlie a stranger!), 'I'll go to bed.'

Stephen knew when he was beaten.

She went to the Hockey dance, though. She and Stephen and Charlie and his young sister, aged seventeen, all descended together to the Town Hall in a brougham. The young girl admired Vera's belt excessively, and looked forward to the moment when she too should be a bewitching and captivating wife like Vera, in short, a woman of the world, worshipped by grave, bearded men. And both the men were under the spell of Vera's incurable charm, capricious, surprising, exasperating, indefinable, indispensable to their lives.

'Stupid superstitions!' reflected Vera. 'But of course I never believed it really.'

And she cast down her eyes to gloat over the belt.

VERA'S SECOND CHRISTMAS ADVENTURE

Curious and strange things had a way of happening to Vera— perhaps because she was an extremely feminine woman. But of all the curious and strange things that ever did happen to Vera, this was certainly the strangest and the most curious. It makes a somewhat exasperating narrative, because the affair ended—or, rather, Vera caused it to end—on a note of interrogation. The reader may, however, draw consolation from the fact that, if he is tormented by an unanswerable query, Vera herself was much more tormented by precisely the same query.

Two days before Christmas, at about three o'clock in the afternoon, just when it was getting dusk and the distant smokepall of the Five Towns was merging in the general greyness of the northern sky, Vera was sitting in the bow-window of the drawing- room of Stephen Cheswardine's newly-acquired house at Sneyd; Sneyd being the fashionable suburb of the Five Towns, graced by the near presence of a countess. And as the slim, thirty-year-old Vera sat there, moody (for reasons which will soon appear), in her charming teagown, her husband drove up to the door in the dogcart, and he was not alone. He had with him a man of vigorous and dashing appearance, fair, far from ugly, and with a masterful face, keen eyes, and most magnificent furs round about him. At sight of the visitor Vera's heart did not exactly jump, but it nearly jumped.

Presently, Stephen brought his acquaintance into the drawing- room.

"My wife," said Stephen, rubbing his hands. "Vera, this is Mr Bittenger, of New York. He will give us the pleasure of spending the night here."

And now Vera's little heart really did jump.

She behaved with the delicious wayward grace which she could always command when she chose to command it. No one would have guessed that she had not spoken to Stephen for a week.

'I'm most happy—most happy,' said Mr Bittenger, with a marked accent and a fine complimentary air. And obviously he was most happy. Vera had impressed him. There was nothing surprising in that. She was in the fullness of her powers in that direction.

It is at this point—at the point of the first jumping of Vera's heart—that the tale begins to be uncanny and disturbing. Thus runs the explanation.

During the year Stephen had gradually grown more and more preoccupied with the subject of his own health. The earthenware business was very good, although, of course, manufacturers were complaining just as usual. Trade, indeed, flourished to such an extent that Stephen had pronounced himself to be suffering from nervous strain and overwork. The symptoms of his malady were chiefly connected with the assimilation of food; to be brief, it was dyspepsia. And as Stephen had previously been one of those favoured people who can eat anything at any hour, and arise in the best of health the next day, Stephen was troubled. At last—about August, when he was obliged to give up wine—he had suddenly decided that the grimy air of the Five Towns was bad for him, and that the household should be removed to Sneyd. And removed to Sneyd it accordingly was. The new house was larger and more splendid even than the Cheswardine abode at Bursley. But Vera did not like the change. Vera preferred the town. Nevertheless, she could not openly demur, since Stephen's health was supposed to be at stake.

During the autumn she was tremendously bored at Sneyd. She had practically no audience for her pretty dresses, and her friends would not flock over from Bursley because of the difficulty of getting home at night. Then it was that Vera had the beautiful idea of spending Christmas in Switzerland. Someone had told her about a certain hotel called The Bear, where, on Christmas Day, never less than a hundred well-dressed and wealthy English people sat down to an orthodox Christmas dinner. The notion enchanted her. She decided, definitely, that she and Stephen should do their Christmassing at The Bear, wherever the Bear was. And as she was fully aware of the power of her capricious charm over Stephen, she regarded the excursion as arranged before she had broached it to him.

Stephen refused. He remarked bitterly that the very thought of a mince-tart made him ill; and that he hated 'abroad'.

Vera took her defeat badly.

She pouted. She sulked. She announced that, if she was not to be allowed to do her Christmassing at The Bear, she would not do it anywhere. She indicated that she meant to perish miserably of ennui in the besotted dullness of Sneyd, and that no Christmas- party of any kind should occur in HER house. She ceased to show interest in Stephen's health. She would not speak. In fact, she went too far. One day, in reply to her rude silence, Stephen said: 'Very well, child, if that's your game, I'll play it with you. Except when other people are present, not a word do I speak to you until you have first spoken to me.'

She knew he would abide by that. He was a monster. She hated him. She loathed him (so she said to herself).

That night, in the agony of her distress, she had dreamed a dream. She dreamed that a stranger came to the house. The details were vague, but the stranger had travelled many miles over water. She could not see him distinctly, but she knew that he was quite bald. In spite of his baldness he inspired her with sympathy. He understood her, praised her costumes, and treated a woman as a woman ought to be treated. Then, somehow or other, he was making love to her, the monster Stephen being absent. She was shocked by his making love to her, and she moved a little farther off him on the sofa (he had sat down by her on a vague sort of sofa in a vague sort of room); but still she was thrilled, and she could not feel as wicked as she felt she ought to feel. Then the dream became hazy; it became hazy at the interesting point of her answer to the love-making. A later stage was very clear. Something was afoot between the monster Stephen and the stranger in the dining- room, and she was locked out of the dining-room. It was Christmas night. She knocked frantically at the door, and at last forced it open, and Stephen was lying in the middle of the floor; the table had been pushed into a corner. 'I killed him quite by accident,' said the stranger affably. And then he seized her by the hand and ruthlessly dragged her away, away, away; and they travelled in trains and ships and trains, and they came to a very noisy, clanging sort of city—and Vera woke up. It had been a highly realistic dream, and it made a deep impression on Vera.

Can one wonder that Vera's heart, being a superstitious little heart, like all our hearts, should leap when the very next day Stephen turned up with a completely unexpected stranger from New York? Of course, dreams are nonsense! Of course! Still—

She did not know whether to rejoice or mourn over the fact that Mr Bittenger was not bald. He was decidedly unbald; he had a glorious shock of chestnut hair. That hair of his naturally destroyed any possible connection with the dream. None the less the coincidence was bizarre.

II

That evening, before dinner, Vera, busy in her chamber beautifying her charms for the ravishment of men from New York, waited with secret anxiety for the arrival of Stephen in his dressing-room. And whereas she usually closed the door between the bedroom and the dressing-room, on this occasion she carefully left it wide open. Stephen came at last. And she waited, listening to his movements in the dressing-room. Not a word! She made brusque movements in the bedroom to attract his attention; she even dropped a brush on the floor. Not a word! After a few moments, she actually ventured into the dressing-room. Stephen was wiping his face, and he glanced at her momentarily over the towel, which hid his nose and mouth. Not a word! And how hard was the monster's glance! She felt that Stephen was one of your absurd literal persons. He had said that he would not speak to her until she had first spoken to him—that was to say in private—public performances did not count. And he would stick to his text, no matter how deliciously she behaved.

She left the dressing-room in haste. Very well! Very well! If Stephen wished for war, he should have it. Her grievance against him grew into something immense. Before, it had been nothing but a kind of two-roomed cottage. She now erected it into a town hall, with imposing portals, and many windows and rich statuary, and suite after suite of enormous rooms, and marble staircases, and lifts that went up and down. She wished she had never married him. She wished that Mr Bittenger HAD been bald.

At dinner everything went with admirable smoothness. Mr Bittenger sat betwixt them. And utmost politeness reigned. In their quality of well-bred hosts, they both endeavoured to keep Mr Bittenger at his ease despite their desolating quarrel; and they entirely succeeded. As the champagne disappeared (and it was not Stephen that drank it), Mr Bittenger became more than at his ease. He was buyer for an important firm of earthenware dealers in New York (Vera had suspected as much—these hospitalities to American buyers are an essential part of business in the Five Towns), and he related very drolly the series of chances or mischances that had left him stranded in England at that season so unseasonable for buying. Vera reflected upon the series of chances or mischances, and upon her dream of the man from over the long miles of water. Of course, dreams are nonsense.... But still—

The conversation passed to the topic of Stephen's health, as conversations in Stephen's house had a habit of doing. Mr Bittenger listened with grave interest.

'I know, I know!' said Mr Bittenger. 'I used to be exactly the same. I guess I understand how you feel—SOME! Don't I?'

'And you are cured?' Stephen demanded, eagerly, as he nibbled at dry toast.

'You bet I'm cured!' said Mr Bittenger.

'You must tell me about that,' said Stephen, and added, 'some time tonight.' He did not care to discuss the bewildering internal economy of the human frame at his dinner-table. There were details...and Mr Bittenger was in a mood that it was no exaggeration to describe as gay.

Shortly afterwards, there arose a discussion as to their respective ages. They coquetted for a few moments, as men invariably will, each diffident about giving away the secret, each asserting that the other was younger than himself.

'Well,' said Mr Bittenger to Vera, at length, 'what age should you give me?'

'I—I should give you five years less than Stephen,' Vera replied.

'And may I ask just how old you are?' Mr Bittenger put the question at close range to Stephen, and hit him full in the face with it.

'I'm forty,' said Stephen.

'So am I!' said Mr Bittenger.

'Well, you don't look it,' said Stephen.

'Sure!' Mr Bittenger admitted, pleased.

'My husband's hair is turning grey,' said Vera, 'while yours—'

'Turning grey!' exclaimed Mr Bittender. 'I wish mine was. I'd give five thousand dollars today if mine was.'

'But why—?' Vera smiled.

'Look here, my dear lady,' said Mr Bittenger, in a peculiar voice, putting down his glass.

And with a swift movement he lifted a wig of glorious chestnut hair from his head—just lifted it for an instant, and dropped it. The man was utterly and completely bald.

III

Vera did nothing foolish. She neither cried, screamed, turned deadly pale, clenched her fragile hands, bit her lips till the blood came, smashed a wine-glass, nor fell with a dull thud senseless to the floor. Nevertheless, she was extremely perturbed by this astounding revelation of Mr Bittenger's. Of course, dreams are nonsense. But still—The truth is, one tries to believe that dreams are nonsense, and up to a certain point one may succeed in believing. But it seemed to Vera that circumstances had passed that point. She could not but admit, also, that if the dream went on being fulfilled, within forty-eight hours Mr Bittenger would have made love to her, and would have killed her husband.

She was so incensed against Stephen that she really could not decide whether she wanted the dream to be fulfilled or not. No one would have imagined that that soft breast could conceal a homicidal thought. Yet so it was. That pretty and delightful woman, wandering about in the edifice of her terrific grievance against Stephen, could not say positively to herself that she would not care to have Stephen killed as a punishment for his sins.

After dinner, she found an excuse for retiring. She must think the puzzle out in solitude. Matters were really going too far. She allowed it to be understood that she was indisposed. Mr Bittenger was full of sorrow and sympathy. But did Stephen show the slightest concern? Stephen did not. She went upstairs, and she meditated, stretched on the sofa at the foot of the bed, a rug over her knees and the fire glinting on her face. Yes, it was her duty as a Christian, if not as an outraged wife, to warn Stephen that the shadow of death was creeping up behind him. He ought at least to be warned. But how could she warn him? Clearly she could not warn him in the presence of Mr Bittenger, the prospective murderer. She would, therefore, have to warn him when they were alone. And that meant that she would have to give way in the great conjugal sulking match. No, never! It was impossible that she should give way there! She frowned desperately at the leaping flames, and did ultimately decide that Stephen's death was preferable to her defeat in that contest. Of such is human nature.

After all, dreams were nonsense.

Surely Stephen would come upstairs to inquire about her health, her indisposition? But no! He came not. And, as he continued not to come, she went downstairs again and proclaimed that she was better.

And then she learned that she had been worrying herself to no purpose whatever. Mr Bittenger was leaving on the morrow, the morrow being Christmas Eve. Stephen would drive him to Bursley in the morning. He would go to the Five Towns Hotel to get his baggage, and catch the Liverpool express at noon. He had booked a passage on the Saxonia, which sailed at threethirty o'clock. Thus he would spend his Christmas at sea; and, spending his Christmas at sea, he could not possibly kill Stephen in the village of Sneyd on Christmas night.

Relief! And yet a certain vague regret in the superstitious little heart! The little heart went to bed again. And Stephen and the stranger stayed up talking very late—doubtless about the famous cure.

The leave-taking the next morning increased the vague regret. Mr Bittenger was the possessor of an attractive individuality, and Vera pondered upon its attractiveness far into the afternoon. How nicely Mr Bittenger had thanked her for her gracious hospitality— with what meaning he had charged the expression of his deep regret at leaving her!

After all, dreams WERE nonsense.

She was sitting in the bow-window of the drawing-room, precisely as she had been sitting twenty-four hours previously, when whom should she see, striding masculinely along the drive towards the house, but Mr Bittenger?

This time she was much more perturbed even than she had been by the revelation of Mr Bittenger's baldness.

After all—

She uprose, the blood having rushed to her head, and retreated she knew not whither, blindly, without a purpose. And found herself in a little morning-room which was scarcely ever used, at the end of the hall. She had not shut the door. And Mr Bittenger, having been admitted by a servant, caught sight of her, and breezily entered her retreat, clad in his magnificent furs.

And as he doffed the furs, he gaily told her what had happened. Owing to difficulties with the Cheswardine mare on the frosty, undulating road between Sneyd and Bursley, and owing to delays with his baggage at the Five Towns Hotel, he had just missed the Liverpool express, and, therefore, the steamer also. He had returned to Stephen's manufactory. Stephen had insisted that he should spend his Christmas with them. And, in brief, there he was. He had walked from Bursley. Stephen, kept by business, was coming later, and so was some of the baggage.

Mr Bittenger's face radiated joy. The loss of his twenty-guinea passage on the Saxonia did not appear to cause him the least regret.

And he sat down by the side of Vera.

And Vera suddenly noticed that they were on a sofa—the sofa of her dream—and she fancied she recognized the room.

'You know, my dear lady,' said Mr Bittenger, looking her straight in the eyes, 'I'm just GLAD I missed my steamer. It gives me a chance to spend a Christmas in England, and in your delightful society—your delightful society—' He gazed at her, without adding to the sentence.

If this was not love-making on a sofa, what could be?

Mr Bittenger had certainly missed the Liverpool express on purpose. Of that Vera was convinced. Or, if he had not missed it on purpose, he had missed it under the dictates of the mysterious power of the dream. Those people who chose to believe that dreams are nonsense were at liberty to do so.

IV

So that in spite of Vera's definite proclamation that there should be no Christmassing in her house that year, Christmassing there emphatically was. Impossible to deny anything to Mr Bittenger! Mr Bittenger wanted holly, the gardener supplied it. Mr Bittenger wanted mistletoe, a bunch of it was brought home by Stephen in the dogcart. Mr Bittenger could not conceive an English Christmas without turkey, mince-pies, plum-pudding, and all the usual indigestiveness. Vera, speaking in a voice which seemed somehow not to be hers, stated that these necessaries of Christmas life would be produced, and Stephen did not say that the very thought of a mince-tart made him ill. Even the English weather, which, it is notorious, has of late shown a sad disposition to imitate, and even to surpass, in mildness the weather of the Riviera at Christmas, decided to oblige Mr Bittenger. At nightfall on Christmas Eve it began to snow gently, but steadily—fine, frozen snow. And the waits, consisting of boys and girls from the Countess of Chell's celebrated institute close by, came and sang in the garden in the falling snow, by the light of a lantern. And Mr Bittenger's heart was as full as it could hold of English Christmas.

As for Vera's heart, it was full of she knew not what. Mr Bittenger's attitude towards her grew more and more chivalrous. He contrived to indicate that he regarded all the years he had spent before making the acquaintance of Vera as so many years absolutely wasted. And Stephen did not seem to care.

They retired to rest that evening up a staircase whose banisters the industrious hands of Mr Bittenger had entwined with holly and paper festoons, and bade each other a merry Christmas with immense fervour; but in the conjugal chamber Stephen maintained his policy of implacable silence. And, naturally, Vera maintained hers. Could it be expected of her that she should yield? The fault was all Stephen's. He ought to have taken her to The Bear, Switzerland. Then there would have been no dream, no Mr Bittenger, and no danger. But as things were, within twenty-four hours he would be a dead man.

And throughout Christmas Day Vera, beneath the gaiety with which she met the vivacious sallies of Mr Bittenger, waited in horrible suspense for the dream to fulfil itself. Stephen alone observed her agitated condition. Stephen said to himself: 'The quarrel is getting on her nerves. She'll yield before she's a day older. It will do her good. Then I'll make it up to her handsomely. But she must yield first.'

He little knew he was standing on the edge of the precipice of death.

The Christmas dinner succeeded admirably; and Stephen, in whom courage was seldom lacking, ate half a mince-pie. The day was almost over. No premature decease had so far occurred. And when both the men said that, if Vera permitted, they would come with her at once to the drawing-room and smoke there, Vera decided that after all dreams were nonsense. She entered the drawing-room first, and Mr Bittenger followed her, with Stephen behind; but just as Stephen was crossing the mat the gardener, holding a parcel in his hands and looking rather strange there in the hall, spoke to him. And Stephen stopped and called to Mr Bittenger. And the drawing-room door was closed upon Vera.

She waited, solitary, for an incredible space of time, and then, having heard unaccustomed and violent sounds in the distance, she could contain herself no longer, and she rang the bell.

'Louisa,' she demanded of the parlourmaid, 'where is your master?'

'Oh, ma'am,' replied Louisa, giggling—a little licence was surely permissible to the girl on Christmas night—'Oh, ma'am, there's such a to-do! Tinsley has just brought some boxing-gloves, and master and Mr Bittenger have got their coats off in the dining- room. And they've had the table pushed up by the door, and you never saw such a set-out in all your life ma'am.'

Vera dismissed Louisa.

There it was—the dream! They were going to box. Mr Bittenger was doubtless an expert, and she knew that Stephen was not. A chance blow by Mr Bittenger in some vital part, and Stephen would be lying stretched in eternal stillness in the middle of the dining- room floor where the table ought to be! The life of the monster was at stake! The life of the brute was in her hands! The dream was fulfilling itself to the point of tragedy!

She jumped up and rushed to the dining-room door. It would not open. Again, the dream!

'You can't come in,' cried Stephen, laughing. 'Wait a bit.'

She pushed against the door, working the handle.

She was about to insist upon the door being opened, when the idea of the danger of such a proceeding occurred to her. In the dream, when she got the door opened, her husband's death had already happened!

Frantically she ran to the kitchen.

'Louisa,' she ordered. 'Go into the garden and tap at the dining- room window, and tell your master that I must speak to him at once in the drawing-room.'

And in a pitiable state of excitation, she returned to the drawing-room.

After another interminable period of suspense, her ear caught the sound of the opening of doors, and then Stephen came into the drawing-room. A singular apparition! He was coatless, as Louisa had said, and the extremities of his long arms were bulged out with cream-coloured boxing-gloves.

She sprang at him and kissed him.

'Steve,' she said, 'are we friends?'

'I should think we were!' he replied, returning her kiss heartily. He had won.

'What are you doing?' she asked him.

'Bittenger and I are just going to have a real round with the gloves. It's part of his cure for my indigestion, you know. He says there's nothing like it. I've only just been able to get gloves. Tinsley brought them up just now. And so we sort of thought we'd like to have a go at once.'

'Why wouldn't you let me into the dining-room?'

'My child, the table was up against the door. And I fancied, perhaps, you wouldn't be exactly charmed, so I—'

'Stephen,' she said, in her most persuasive voice, 'will you do something to please me?'

'What is it?'

'Will you?'

A pause.

'Yes, certainly.'

'Don't box tonight.'

'Oh—well! What will Bittenger think?'

Another pause.

'Never mind! You don't want me to box, really?'

'I don't want you to box—not tonight.' 'Agreed, my chuck!' And he kissed her again. He could well afford to be magnanimous.

Mr Bittenger ploughed the seas alone to New York.

But supposing that Vera had not interfered, what would have happened? That is the unanswerable query which torments the superstitious little brain of Vera.

THE BURGLARY

I

Lady Dain said: 'Jee, if that portrait stays there much longer, you'll just have to take me off to Pirehill one of these fine mornings.'

Pirehill is the seat of the great local hospital; but it is also the seat of the great local lunatic asylum; and when the inhabitants of the Five Towns say merely 'Pirehill', they mean the asylum.

'I do declare I can't fancy my food now-a-days,' said Lady Dain, 'and it's all that portrait!' She stared plaintively up at the immense oil-painting which faced her as she sat at the breakfast- table in her spacious and opulent dining-room.

Sir Jehoshaphat made no remark.

Despite Lady Dain's animadversions upon it, despite the undoubted fact that it was generally disliked in the Five Towns, the portrait had cost a thousand pounds (some said guineas), and though not yet two years old it was probably worth at least fifteen hundred in the picture market. For it was a Cressage; and not only was it a Cressage—it was one of the finest Cressages in existence.

It marked the summit of Sir Jehoshaphat's career. Sir Jehoshaphat's career was, perhaps, the most successful and brilliant in the entire social history of the Five Towns. This famous man was the principal partner in Dain Brothers. His brother was dead, but two of Sir Jee's sons were in the firm. Dain Brothers were the largest manufacturers of cheap earthenware in the district, catering chiefly for the American and Colonial buyer. They had an extremely bad reputation for cutting prices. They were hated by every other firm in the Five Towns, and, to hear rival manufacturers talk, one would gather the impression that Sir Jee had acquired a tremendous fortune by systematically selling goods under cost. They were also hated by between eighteen and nineteen hundred employees. But such hatred, however virulent, had not marred the progress of Sir Jee's career.

He had meant to make a name and he had made it. The Five Towns might laugh at his vulgar snobbishness. The Five Towns might sneer at his calculated philanthropy. But he was, nevertheless, the best-known man in the Five Towns, and it was precisely his snobbishness and his philanthropy which had carried him to the top. Moreover, he had been the first public man in the Five Towns to gain a knighthood. The Five Towns could not deny that it was very proud indeed of this knighthood. The means by which he had won this distinction were neither here nor there—he had won it. And was he not the father of his native borough? Had he not been three times mayor of his native borough? Was not the whole northern half of the county dotted and spangled by his benefactions, his institutions, his endowments?

And it could not be denied that he sometimes tickled the Five Towns as the Five Towns likes being tickled. There was, for example, the notorious Sneyd incident. Sneyd Hall, belonging to the Earl of Chell, lies a few miles south of the Five Towns, and from it the pretty Countess of Chell exercises that condescending meddlesomeness which so frequently exasperates the Five Towns.

Sir Jee had got his title by the aid of the Countess-'Interfering Iris', as she is locally dubbed. Shortly afterwards he had contrived to quarrel with the Countess; and the quarrel was conducted by Sir Jee as a quarrel between equals, which delighted the district. Sir Jee's final word in it had been to buy a sizable tract of land near Sneyd village, just off the Sneyd estate, and to erect thereon a mansion quite as imposing as Sneyd Hall, and far more up to date, and to call the mansion Sneyd Castle. A mighty stroke! Iris was furious; the Earl speechless with fury. But they could do nothing. Naturally the Five Towns was tickled.

It was apropos of the house-warming of Sneyd Castle, also of the completion of his third mayoralty, and of the inauguration of the Dain Technical Institute, that the movement had been started (primarily by a few toadies) for tendering to Sir Jee a popular gift worthy to express the profound esteem in which he was officially held in the Five Towns. It having been generally felt that the gift should take the form of a portrait, a local dilettante had suggested Cressage, and when the Five Towns had inquired into Cressage and discovered that that genius from the United States was celebrated throughout the civilized world, and regarded as the equal of Velazquez (whoever Velazquez might be), and that he had painted half the aristocracy, and that his income was regal, the suggestion was accepted and Cressage was approached.

Cressage haughtily consented to paint Sir Jee's portrait on his usual conditions; namely, that the sitter should go to the little village in Bedfordshire where Cressage had his principal studio, and that the painting should be exhibited at the Royal Academy before being shown anywhere else. (Cressage was an R.A., but no one thought of putting R.A. after his name. He was so big, that instead of the Royal Academy conferring distinction on him, he conferred distinction on the Royal Academy.)

Sir Jee went to Bedfordshire and was rapidly painted, and he came back gloomy. The presentation committee went to Bedfordshire later to inspect the portrait, and they, too, came back gloomy.

Then the Academy Exhibition opened, and the portrait, showing Sir Jee in his robe and chain and in a chair, was instantly hailed as possibly the most glorious masterpiece of modern times. All the critics were of one accord. The committee and Sir Jee were reassured, but only partially, and Sir Jee rather less so than the committee. For there was something in the enthusiastic criticism which gravely disturbed him. An enlightened generation, thoroughly familiar with the dazzling yearly succession of Cressage's portraits, need not be told what this something was. One critic wrote that Cressage displayed even more than his 'customary astounding insight into character....' Another critic wrote that Cressage's observation was, as usual, 'calmly and coldly hostile'. Another referred to the 'typical provincial mayor, immortalized for the diversion of future ages.'

Inhabitants of the Five Towns went to London to see the work for which they had subscribed, and they saw a mean, little, old man, with thin lips and a straggling grey beard, and shifty eyes, and pushful snob written all over him; ridiculous in his gewgaws of office. When you looked at the picture close to, it was a meaningless mass of coloured smudges, but when you stood fifteen feet away from it the portrait was absolutely lifelike, amazing, miraculous. It was so wondrously lifelike that some of the inhabitants of the Five Towns burst out laughing. Many people felt sorry—not for Sir Jee—but for Lady Dain. Lady Dain was beloved and genuinely respected. She was a simple, homely, sincere woman, her one weakness being that she had never been able to see through Sir Jee.

Of course, at the presentation ceremony the portrait had been ecstatically referred to as a possession precious for ever, and the recipient and his wife pretended to be overflowing with pure joy in the ownership of it.

It had been hanging in the dining-room of Sneyd Castle about sixteen months, when Lady Dain told her husband that it would ultimately drive her into the lunatic asylum.

'Don't be silly, wife,' said Sir Jee. 'I wouldn't part with that portrait for ten times what it cost.'

This was, to speak bluntly, a downright lie. Sir Jee secretly hated the portrait more than anyone hated it. He would have been almost ready to burn down Sneyd Castle in order to get rid of the thing. But it happened that on the previous evening, in the conversation with the magistrates' clerk, his receptive brain had been visited by a less expensive scheme than burning down the castle.

Lady Dain sighed.

'Are you going to town early?' she inquired.

'Yes,' he replied. 'I'm on the rota today.'

He was chairman of the borough Bench of magistrates. As he drove into town he revolved his scheme and thought it wild and dangerous, but still feasible.

II

On the Bench that morning Sir Jee shocked Mr Sherratt, the magistrates' clerk, and he utterly disgusted Mr Bourne, superintendent of the borough police. (I do not intend to name the name of the borough—whether Bursley, Hanbridge, Knype, Longshaw, or Turnhill. The inhabitants of the Five Towns will know without being told; the rest of the world has no right to know.) There had recently occurred a somewhat thrilling series of burglaries in the district, and the burglars (a gang of them was presumed) had escaped the solicitous attentions of the police. But on the previous afternoon an underling of Mr Bourne's had caught a man who was generally believed to be wholly or partly responsible for the burglaries. The Five Towns breathed with relief and congratulated Mr Bourne; and Mr Bourne was well pleased with himself. The Staffordshire Signal headed the item of news, 'Smart Capture of a Supposed Burglar'. The supposed burglar gave his name as William Smith, and otherwise behaved in an extremely suspicious manner.

Now, Sir Jee, sitting as chief magistrate in the police-court, actually dismissed the charge against the man! Overruling his sole colleague on the Bench that morning, Alderman Easton, he dismissed the charge against William Smith, holding that the evidence for the prosecution was insufficient to justify even a remand. No wonder that Mr Bourne was discouraged, not to say angry. No wonder that that pillar of the law, Mr Sherratt, was pained and shocked. At the conclusion of the case Sir Jehoshaphat said that he would be glad to speak with William Smith afterwards in the magistrates' room, indicating that he sympathized with William Smith, and wished to exercise upon William Smith his renowned philanthropy.

And so, at about noon, when the Court majestically rose, Sir Jee retired to the magistrates' room, where the humble Alderman Easton was discreet enough not to follow him, and awaited William Smith. And William Smith came, guided thither by a policeman, to whom, in parting from him, he made a rude, surreptitious gesture.

Sir Jee, seated in the arm-chair which dominates the other chairs round the elm table in the magistrates' room, emitted a preliminary cough.

'Smith,' he said sternly, leaning his elbows on the table, 'you were very fortunate this morning, you know.'

And he gazed at Smith.

Smith stood near the door, cap in hand. He did not resemble a burglar, who surely ought to be big, muscular, and masterful. He resembled an undersized clerk who has been out of work for a long time, but who has nevertheless found the means to eat and drink rather plenteously. He was clothed in a very shabby navy-blue suit, frayed at the wrists and ankles, and greasy in front. His linen collar was brown with dirt, his fingers were dirty, his hair was unkempt and long, and a young and lusty black beard was sprouting on his chin. His boots were not at all pleasant.

'Yes, governor,' Smith replied, lightly, with a Manchester accent. 'And what's YOUR game?'

Sir Jee was taken aback. He, the chairman of the borough Bench, and the leading philanthropist in the country, to be so spoken to! But what could he do? He himself had legally established Smith's innocence. Smith was as free as air, and had a perfect right to adopt any tone he chose to any man he chose. And Sir Jee desired a service from William Smith.

'I was hoping I might be of use to you,' said Sir Jehoshaphat diplomatically.

'Well,' said Smith, 'that's all right, that is. But none of your philanthropic dodges, you know. I don't want to lead a new life, and I don't want to turn over a new leaf, and I don't want a helpin' hand, nor none o' those things. And, what's more, I don't want a situation. I've got all the situation as I need. But I never refuse money, nor beer neither. Never did, and I'm forty years old next month.'

'I suppose burgling doesn't pay very well, does it?' Sir Jee boldly ventured.

William Smith laughed coarsely.

'It pays right enough,' said he. 'But I don't put my money on my back, governor, I put it into a bit of public-house property when I get the chance.'

'It may pay,' said Sir Jee. 'But it is wrong. It is very anti-social.'

'Is it, indeed?' Smith returned dryly. 'Anti-social, is it? Well, I've heard it called plenty o' things in my time, but never that. Now, I should have called it quite sociablelike, sort of making free with strangers, and so on. However,' he added, 'I come across a cove once as told me crime was nothing but a disease and ought to be treated as such. I asked him for a dozen o' port, but he never sent it.'

'Ever been caught before?' Sir Jee inquired.

'Not much!' Smith exclaimed. 'And this'll be a lesson to me, I can tell you. Now, what are you getting at, governor? Because my time's money, my time is.'

Sir Jee coughed once more.

'Sit down,' said Sir Jee.

And William Smith sat down opposite to him at the table, and put his shiny elbows on the table precisely in the manner of Sir Jee's elbows.

'Well?' he cheerfully encouraged Sir Jee.

'How would you like to commit a burglary that was not a crime?' said Sir Jee, his shifty eyes wandering around the room. 'A perfectly lawful burglary?'

'What ARE you getting at?' William Smith was genuinely astonished.

'At my residence, Sneyd Castle,' Sir Jee proceeded, 'there's a large portrait of myself in the dining-room that I want to have stolen. You understand?'

'Stolen?'

'Yes. I want to get rid of it. And I want—er—people to think that it has been stolen.'

'Well, why don't you stop up one night and steal it yourself, and then burn it?' William Smith suggested.

'That would be deceitful,' said Sir Jee, gravely. 'I could not tell my friends that the portrait had been stolen if it had not been stolen. The burglary must be entirely genuine.'

'What's the figure?' said Smith curtly.

'Figure?'

'What are you going to give me for the job?'

'GIVE you for doing the job?' Sir Jee repeated, his secret and ineradicable meanness aroused. 'GIVE you? Why, I'm giving you the opportunity to honestly steal a picture that's worth over a thousand pounds—I dare say it would be worth two thousand pounds in America—and you want to be paid into the bargain! Do you know, my man, that people come all the way from Manchester, and even London, to see that portrait?' He told Smith about the painting.

'Then why are you in such a stew to be rid of it?' queried the burglar.

'That's my affair,' said Sir Jee. 'I don't like it. Lady Dain doesn't like it. But it's a presentation portrait, and so I can't— you see, Mr Smith?'

'And how am I going to dispose of it when I've got it?' Smith demanded. 'You can't melt a portrait down as if it was silver. By what you say, governor, it's known all over the blessed world. Seems to me I might just as well try to sell the Nelson Column.'

'Oh, nonsense!' said Sir Jee. 'Nonsense. You'll sell it in America quite easily. It'll be a fortune to you. Keep it for a year first, and then send it to New York.'

William Smith shook his head and drummed his fingers on the table; and then quite suddenly he brightened and said—

'All right, governor. I'll take it on, just to oblige you.'

'When can you do it?' asked Sir Jee, hardly concealing his joy. 'Tonight?'

'No,' said Smith, mysteriously. 'I'm engaged tonight.'

'Well, tomorrow night?'

'Nor tomorrow. I'm engaged tomorrow too.'

'You seem to be very much engaged, my man,' Sir Jee observed.

'What do you expect?' Smith retorted. 'Business is business. I could do it the night after tomorrow.'

'But that's Christmas Eve,' Sir Jee protested.

'What if it is Christmas Eve?' said Smith coldly. 'Would you prefer Christmas Day? I'm engaged on Boxing Day AND the day after.'

'Not in the Five Towns, I trust?' Sir Jee remarked.

'No,' said Smith shortly. 'The Five Towns is about sucked dry.'

The affair was arranged for Christmas Eve.

'Now,' Sir Jee suggested, 'shall I draw you a plan of the castle, so that you can—'

William Smith's face expressed terrific scorn. 'Do you suppose,' he said, 'as I haven't had plans o' your castle ever since it was built? What do you take me for? I'm not a blooming excursionist, I'm not. I'm a business man—that's what I am.'

Sir Jee was snubbed, and he agreed submissively to all William Smith's arrangements for the innocent burglary. He perceived that in William Smith he had stumbled on a professional of the highest class, and this good fortune pleased him.

'There's only one thing that riles me,' said Smith, in parting, 'and that is that you'll go and say that after you'd done everything you could for me I went and burgled your castle. And you'll talk about the ingratitude of the lower classes. I know you, governor!'

III

On the afternoon of the 24th of December Sir Jehoshaphat drove home to Sneyd Castle from the principal of the three Dain manufactories, and found Lady Dain superintending the work of packing up trunks. He and she were to quit the castle that afternoon in order to spend Christmas on the other side of the Five Towns, under the roof of their eldest son, John, who had a new house, a new wife, and a new baby (male). John was a domineering person, and, being rather proud of his house and all that was his, he had obstinately decided to have his own Christmas at his own hearth. Grandpapa and Grandmamma, drawn by the irresistible attraction of that novelty, a grandson (though Mrs John HAD declined to have the little thing named Jehoshaphat), had yielded to John's solicitations, and the family gathering, for the first time in history, was not to occur round Sir Jee's mahogany.

Sir Jee, very characteristically, said nothing to Lady Dain immediately. He allowed her to proceed with the packing of the trunks, and then tea was served, and as the time was approaching for the carriage to come round to take them to the station, at last he suddenly remarked-

'I shan't be able to go with you to John's this afternoon.'

'Oh, Jee!' she exclaimed. 'Really, you are tiresome. Why couldn't you tell me before?'

'I will come over tomorrow morning—perhaps in time for church,' he proceeded, ignoring her demand for an explanation.

He always did ignore her demand for an explanation. Indeed, she only asked for explanations in a mechanical and perfunctory manner—she had long since ceased to expect them. Sir Jee had been born like that—devious, mysterious, incalculable. And Lady Dain accepted him as he was. She was somewhat surprised, therefore, when he went on—

'I have some minutes of committee meetings that I really must go carefully through and send off tonight, and you know as well as I do that there'll be no chance of doing that at John's. I've telegraphed to John.'

He was obviously nervous and self-conscious.

'There's no food in the house,' sighed Lady Dain. 'And the servants are all going away except Callear, and HE can't cook your dinner tonight. I think I'd better stay myself and look after you.'

'You'll do no such thing,' said Sir Jee, decisively. 'As for my dinner, anything will do for that. The servants have been promised their holiday, to start from this evening, and they must have it. I can manage.'

Here spoke the philanthropist with his unshakable sense of justice.

So Lady Dain departed, anxious and worried, having previously arranged something cold for Sir Jee in the dining-room, and instructed Callear about boiling the water for Sir Jee's tea on Christmas morning. Callear was the under-coachman and a useful odd man. He it was who would drive Sir Jee to the station on Christmas morning, and then guard the castle and the stables thereof during the absence of the family and the other servants. Callear slept over the stables.

And after Sir Jee had consumed his cold repast in the dining-room the other servants went, and Sir Jee was alone in the castle, facing the portrait.

He had managed the affair fairly well, he thought. Indeed, he had a talent for chicane, and none knew it better than himself. It would have been dangerous if the servants had been left in the castle. They might have suffered from insomnia, and heard William Smith, and interfered with the operations of William Smith. On the other hand, Sir Jee had no intention whatever of leaving the castle uninhabited to the mercies of William Smith. He felt that he himself must be on the spot to see that everything went right and that nothing went wrong. Thus, the previously-arranged scheme for the servants' holiday fitted perfectly into his plans, and all that he had had to do was to refuse to leave the castle till the morrow. It was ideal.

Nevertheless, he was a little afraid of what he had done, and of what he was going to permit William Smith to do. It was certainly dangerous—certainly rather a wild scheme. However, the die was cast. And within twelve hours he would be relieved of the intolerable incubus of the portrait.

And when he thought of the humiliations which that portrait had caused him; when he remembered the remarks of his sons concerning it, especially John's remarks; when he recalled phrases about it in London newspapers, he squirmed, and told himself that no scheme for getting rid of it could be too wild and perilous. And, after all, the burglary dodge was the only dodge, absolutely the only conceivable practical method of disposing of the portrait—except burning down the castle. And surely it was preferable to a conflagration, to arson! Moreover, in case of fire at the castle some blundering fool would be sure to cry; 'The portrait! The portrait must be saved!' And the portrait would be saved.

He gazed at the repulsive, hateful thing. In the centre of the lower part of the massive gold frame was the legend: 'Presented to Sir Jehoshaphat Dain, Knight, as a mark of public esteem and gratitude,' etc. He wondered if William Smith would steal the frame. It was to be hoped that he would not steal the frame. In fact, William Smith would find it very difficult to steal that frame unless he had an accomplice or so.

'This is the last time I shall see YOU!' said Sir Jee to the portrait.

Then he unfastened the catch of one of the windows in the dining- room (as per contract with William Smith), turned out the electric light, and went to bed in the deserted castle.

He went to bed, but not to sleep. It was no part of Sir Jee's programme to sleep. He intended to listen, and he did listen.

And about two o'clock, precisely the hour which William Smith had indicated, he fancied he heard muffled and discreet noises. Then he was sure that he heard them. William Smith had kept his word. Then the noises ceased for a period, and then they recommenced. Sir Jee restrained his curiosity as long as he could, and when he could restrain it no more he rose and silently opened his bedroom window and put his head out into the nipping night air of Christmas. And by good fortune he saw the vast oblong of the picture, carefully enveloped in sheets, being passed by a couple of dark figures through the dining-room window to the garden outside. William Smith had a colleague, then, and he was taking the frame as well as the canvas. Sir Jee watched the men disappear down the avenue, and they did not reappear. Sir Jee returned to bed.

Yes, he felt himself equal to facing it out with his family and friends. He felt himself equal to pretending that he had no knowledge of the burglary.

Having slept a few hours, he got up early and, half-dressed, descended to the dining-room just to see what sort of a mess William Smith had made.

The canvas of the portrait lay flat on the hearthrug, with the following words written on it in chalk: 'This is no use to me.' It was the massive gold frame that had gone.

Further, as was later discovered, all the silver had gone. Not a spoon was left in the castle.

NEWS OF THE ENGAGEMENT

My mother never came to meet me at Bursley station when I arrived in the Five Towns from London; much less did she come as far as Knype station, which is the great traffic centre of the district, the point at which one changes from the express into the local train. She had always other things to do; she was 'preparing' for me. So I had the little journey from Knype to Bursley, and then the walk up Trafalgar Road, amid the familiar high chimneys and the smoke and the clayey mud and the football posts and the Midland accent, all by myself. And there was leisure to consider anew how I should break to my mother the tremendous news I had for her. I had been considering that question ever since getting into the train at Euston, where I had said goodbye to Agnes; but in the atmosphere of the Five Towns it seemed just slightly more difficult; though, of course, it wasn't difficult, really.

You see, I wrote to my mother regularly every week, telling her most of my doings. She knew all my friends by name. I dare say she formed in her mind notions of what sort of people they were. Thus I had frequently mentioned Agnes and her family in my letters. But you can't write even to your mother and say in cold blood: 'I think I am beginning to fall in love with Agnes,' 'I think Agnes likes me,' 'I am mad on her,' 'I feel certain she likes me,' 'I shall propose to her on such a day.' You can't do that. At least I couldn't. Hence it had come about that on the 20th of December I had proposed to Agnes and been accepted by Agnes, and my mother had no suspicion that my happiness was so near. And on the 22nd, by a previous and unalterable arrangement, I had come to spend Christmas with my mother.

I was the only son of a widow; I was all that my mother had. And lo! I had gone and engaged myself to a girl she had never seen, and I had kept her in the dark! She would certainly be extremely surprised, and she might be a little bit hurt—just at first. Anyhow, the situation was the least in the world delicate.

I walked up the whitened front steps of my mother's little house, just opposite where the electric cars stop, but before I could put my hand on the bell my little plump mother, in her black silk and her gold brooch and her auburn hair, opened to me, having doubtless watched me down the road from the bay-window, as usual, and she said, as usual kissing me—

'Well, Philip! How are you?'

And I said—

'Oh! I'm all right, mother. How are you?'

I perceived instantly that she was more excited than my arrival ordinarily made her. There were tears in her smiling eyes, and she was as nervous as a young girl. She did indeed look remarkably young for a woman of forty-five, with twenty-five years of widowhood and a brief but too tempestuous married life behind her.

The thought flashed across my mind: 'By some means or other she has got wind of my engagement. But how?'

But I said nothing. I, too, was naturally rather nervous. Mothers are kittle cattle.

'I'll tell her at supper,' I decided.

And she hovered round me, like a sea-gull round a steamer, as I went upstairs.

There was a ring at the door. She flew, instead of letting the servant go. It was a porter with my bag.

Just as I was coming down-stairs again there was another ring at the door. And my mother appeared magically out of the kitchen, but I was beforehand with her, and with a laugh I insisted on opening the front door myself this time. A young woman stood on the step.

'Please, Mrs Dawson wants to know if Mrs Durance can kindly lend her half-a-dozen knives and forks?'

'Eh, with pleasure,' said my mother, behind me. 'Just wait a minute, Lucy. Come inside on the mat.'

I followed my mother into the drawing-room, where she kept her silver in a cabinet.

'That's Mrs Dawson's new servant,' my mother whispered. 'But she needn't think I'm going to lend her my best, because I'm not.'

'I shouldn't, if I were you,' I supported her.

And she went out with some second-best in tissue paper, and beamed on Mrs Dawson's servant with an assumed benevolence.

'There!' she exclaimed. 'And the compliments of the season to your mistress, Lucy.'

After that my mother disappeared into the kitchen to worry an entirely capable servant. And I roamed about, feeling happily excited, examining the drawing-room, in which nothing was changed except the incandescent light and the picture postcards on the mantelpiece. Then I wandered into the dining-room, a small room at the back of the house, and here an immense surprise awaited me.

Supper was set for three!

'Well,' I reflected. 'Here's a nice state of affairs! Supper for three, and she hasn't breathed a word!'

My mother was so clever in social matters, and especially in the planning of delicious surprises, that I believed her capable even of miracles. In some way or other she must have discovered the state of my desires towards Agnes. She had written, or something. She and Agnes had been plotting together by letter to startle me, and perhaps telegraphing. Agnes had fibbed in telling me that she could not possibly come to Bursley for Christmas; she had delightfully fibbed. And my mother had got her concealed somewhere in the house, or was momentarily expecting her. That explained the tears, the nervousness, the rushes to the door.

I crept out of the dining-room, determined not to let my mother know that I had secretly viewed the supper-table. And as I was crossing the lobby to the drawing-room there was a third ring at the door, and a third time my mother rushed out of the kitchen.

'By Jove!' I thought. 'Suppose it's Agnes. What a scene!'

And trembling with expectation I opened the door. It was Mr Nixon.

Now, Mr Nixon was an old friend of the family's, a man of forty- nine or fifty, with a reputation for shrewdness and increasing wealth. He owned a hundred and seventy-five cottages in the town, having bought them gradually in half-dozens, and in rows; he collected the rents himself, and attended to the repairs himself, and was celebrated as a good landlord, and as being almost the only man in Bursley who had made cottage property pay. He lived alone in Commerce Street, and, though not talkative, was usually jolly, with one or two good stories tucked away in the corners of his memory. He was my mother's trustee, and had morally aided her in the troublous times before my father's early death.

'Well, young man,' cried he. 'So you're back in owd Bosley!' It amused him to speak the dialect a little occasionally.

And he brought his burly, powerful form into the lobby.

I greeted him as jovially as I could, and then he shook hands with my mother, neither of them speaking.

'Mr Nixon is come for supper, Philip,' said my mother.

I liked Mr Nixon, but I was not too well pleased by this information, for I wanted to talk confidentially to my mother. I had a task before me with my mother, and here Mr Nixon was plunging into the supper. I could not break it gently to my mother that I was engaged to a strange young woman in the presence of Mr Nixon. Mr Nixon had been in to supper several times during previous visits of mine, but never on the first night.

However, I had to make the best of it. And we sat down and began on the ham, the sausages, the eggs, the crumpets, the toast, the jams, the mince-tarts, the Stilton, and the celery. But we none of us ate very much, despite my little plump mother's protestations.

My suspicion was that perhaps something had gone slightly wrong with my mother's affairs, and that Mr Nixon was taking the first opportunity to explain things to me. But such a possibility did not interest me, for I could easily afford to keep my mother and a wife too. I was still preoccupied in my engagement—and surely there is nothing astonishing in that—and I began to compose the words in which, immediately on the departure of Mr Nixon after supper, I would tackle my mother on the subject.

When we had reached the Stilton and celery, I intimated that I must walk down to the post-office, as I had to dispatch a letter.

'Won't it do tomorrow, my pet?' asked my mother.

'It will not,' I said.

Imagine leaving Agnes two days without news of my safe arrival and without assurances of my love! I had started writing the letter in the train, near Willesden, and I finished it in the drawing-room.

'A lady in the case?' Mr Nixon called out gaily.

'Yes,' I replied with firmness.

I went forth, bought a picture postcard showing St Luke's Square, Bursley, most untruthfully picturesque, and posted the card and the letter to my darling

Agnes. I hoped that Mr Nixon would have departed ere my return; he had made no reference at all during supper to my mother's affairs. But he had not departed. I found him solitary in the drawing-room, smoking a very fine cigar.

'Where's the mater?' I demanded.

'She's just gone out of the room,' he said. 'Come and sit down. Have a weed. I want a bit of a chat with you, Philip.'

I obeyed, taking one of the very fine cigars.

'Well, Uncle Nixon,' I encouraged him, wishing to get the chat over because my mind was full of Agnes. I sometimes called him uncle for fun.

'Well, my boy,' he began. 'It's no use me beating about the bush. What do you think of me as a stepfather?'

I was struck, as they say down there, all of a heap.

'What?' I stammered. 'You don't mean to say—you and mother—?'

He nodded.

'Yes, I do, lad. Yesterday she promised as she'd marry my unworthy self. It's been coming along for some time. But I don't expect she's given you any hint in her letters. In fact, I know she hasn't. It would have been rather difficult, wouldn't it? She couldn't well have written, "My dear Philip, an old friend, Mr Nixon, is falling in love with me and I believe I'm falling in love with him. One of these days he'll be proposing to me." She couldn't have written like that, could she?'

I laughed. I could not help it.

'Shake hands,' I said warmly. 'I'm delighted.'

And soon afterwards my mother sidled in, shyly.

'The lad's delighted, Sarah,' said Mr Nixon shortly.

I said nothing about my own engagement that night. I had never thought of my mother as a woman with a future, I had never realized that she was desirable, and that a man might desire her, and that her lonely existence in that house was not all that she had the right to demand from life. And I was ashamed of my characteristic filial selfish egoism. So I decided that I would not intrude my joys on hers until the next morning. We live and learn.

BEGINNING THE NEW YEAR

I

We are a stolid and a taciturn race, we of the Five Towns. It may be because we are geographically so self contained; or it may be because we work in clay and iron; or it may merely be because it is our nature to be stolid and taciturn. But stolid and taciturn we are; and some of the instances of our stolidity and our taciturnity are enough to astound. They do not, of course, astound us natives; we laugh at them, we think they are an immense joke, and what the outer world may think does not trouble our deep conceit of ourselves. I have often wondered what would be the effect, other than an effect of astonishment, on the outer world, of one of these narratives illustrating our Five Towns peculiarities of deportment. And I intend for the first time in history to make such a narrative public property. I have purposely not chosen an extreme example; just an average example. You will see how it strikes you.

Toby Hall, once a burgess of Turnhill, the northernmost and smallest of the Five Towns, was passing, last New Year's Eve, through the district by train on his way from Crewe to Derby. He lived at Derby, and he was returning from the funeral of a brother member of the Ancient Order of Foresters at Crewe. He got out of the train at Knype, the great railway centre of the Five Towns, to have a glass of beer in the second-class refreshment-room. It being New Year's Eve, the traffic was heavy and disorganized, especially in the refreshment-room, and when Toby Hall emerged on to the platform again the train was already on the move. Toby was neither young nor active. His years were fifty, and on account of the funeral he wore broadcloth and a silk hat, and his overcoat was new and encumbering. Impossible to take a flying leap into the train! He missed the train. And then he reflectively stroked his short grey beard (he had no moustache, and his upper lip was very long), and then he smoothed down his new overcoat over his rotund form.

'Young man,' he asked a porter. 'When's next train Derby way?'

'Ain't none afore tomorrow.'

Toby went and had another glass of beer.

'D—d if I don't go to Turnhill,' he said to himself, slowly and calmly, as he paid for the second glass of beer.

He crossed the station by the subway and waited for the loop-line train to Turnhill. He had not set foot in the Five Towns for three-and-twenty years, having indeed carefully and continuously avoided it, as a man will avoid the street where his creditor lives. But he discovered no change in Knype railway-station. And he had a sort of pleasure in the fact that he knew his way about it, knew where the loop-line trains started from and other interesting little details. Even the special form of the loop-line time-table, pasted here and there on the walls of the station, had not varied since his youth. (We return Radicals to Parliament, but we are proud of a railway which for fine old English conservatism brooks no rival.)

Toby gazed around, half challengingly and half nervously—it was conceivable that he might be recognized, or might recognize. But no! Not a soul in the vast, swaying, preoccupied, luggage-laden crowds gave him a glance. As for him, although he fully recognized nobody, yet nearly every face seemed to be half-familiar. He climbed into a second-class compartment when the train drew up, and ten other people, all with third-class tickets, followed his example; three persons were already seated therein. The compartment was illuminated by one lamp, and in the Bleakridge Tunnel this lamp expired. Everything reminded him of his youth.

In twenty minutes he was leaving Turnhill station and entering the town. It was about nine o'clock, and colder than winters of the period usually are. The first thing he saw was an electric tram, and the second thing he saw was another electric tram. In Toby's time there were no trams at Turnhill, and the then recently- introduced steam-trams between Bursley and Longshaw, long since superseded, were regarded as the final marvel of science as applied to traction. And now there were electric trams at Turnhill! The railway renewed his youth, but this darting electricity showed him how old he was. The Town Hall, which was brand-new when he left Turnhill, had the look of a mediaeval hotel de ville as he examined it in the glamour of the corporation's incandescent gas. And it was no more the sole impressive pile in the borough. The High Street and its precincts abounded in impressive piles. He did not know precisely what they were, but they had the appearance of being markets, libraries, baths, and similar haunts of luxury; one was a bank. He thought that Turnhill High Street compared very well with Derby. He would have preferred it to be less changed. If the High Street was thus changed, everything would be changed, including Child Row. The sole phenomenon that recalled his youth (except the Town Hall) was the peculiar smell of oranges and apples floating out on the frosty air from holly-decorated greengrocers' shops.

He passed through the Market Square, noting that sinister freak, the Jubilee Tower, and came to Child Row. The first building on your right as you enter Child Row from the square is the Primitive Methodist Chapel. Yes, it was still there; Primitive Methodism had not failed in Turnhill because Toby Hall had deserted the cause three-and-twenty years ago! But something serious had happened to the structure. Gradually Toby realized that its old face had been taken out and a new one put in, the classic pillars had vanished, and a series of Gothic arches had been substituted by way of portico; a pretty idea, but not to Toby's liking. It was another change, another change! He crossed the street and proceeded downwards in the obscurity, and at length halted and peered with his little blue eyes at a small house (one of twins) on the other side from where he stood. That house, at any rate, was unchanged. It was a two-storeyed house, with a semicircular fanlight over a warped door of grained panelling. The blind of the window to the left of the door was irradiated from within, proving habitation.

'I wonder—' ran Toby's thought. And he unhesitatingly crossed the street again, towards it, feeling first for the depth of the kerbstone with his umbrella. He had a particular and special interest in that house (No. 11 it was—and is), for, four-and- twenty years ago he had married it. II

Four-and-twenty years ago Toby Hall (I need not say that his proper Christian name was Tobias) had married Miss Priscilla Bratt, then a calm and self-reliant young woman of twenty-three, and Priscilla had the house, together with a certain income, under the will of her father. The marriage was not the result of burning passion on either side. It was a union of two respectabilities, and it might have succeeded as well as such unions generally do succeed, if Priscilla had not too frequently mentioned the fact that the house they lived in was hers. He knew that the house was hers. The whole world was perfectly aware of the ownership of the house, and her references to the matter amounted to a lack of tact. Several times Toby had indicated as much. But Priscilla took no heed. She had the hide of an alligator herself (though a personable girl), and she assumed that her husband's hide was of similar stuff. This assumption was justifiable, except that in just one spot the skin of Toby was tender. He really did not care to be reminded that he was living under his wife's roof. The reiteration settled on his nerves like a malady. And before a year had elapsed Priscilla had contrived to remind him once too often. And one day he put some things in a carpet-bag, and a hat on his head, and made for the door. The house was antique, and the front- parlour gave directly on to the street.

'Where be going?' Priscilla asked him.

He hesitated a second, and said—

'Merica.'

And he was. In the Five Towns we are apt to end our marriages in that laconic manner. Toby did not complain too much; he simply and unaffectedly went. It might be imagined that the situation was a trying one for Priscilla. Not so! Priscilla had experienced marriage with Toby and had found it wanting. She was content to be relieved of Toby. She had her house and her money and her self-esteem, and also tranquillity. She accepted the solution, and devoted her days to the cleanliness of the house.

Toby drew all the money he had out of the Bursley and Turnhill Permanent Fifty Pounds Benefit Building Society (four shares, nearly paid up) and set sail—in the Adriatic, which was then the leading greyhound of the Atlantic—for New York. From New York he went to Trenton (New Jersey), which is the Five Towns of America. A man of his skill in handling clay on a wheel had no difficulty whatever in wresting a good livelihood from Trenton. When he had tarried there a year he caused a letter to be written to his wife informing her that he was dead. He wished to be quite free; and also (we have our feeling for justice) he wished his wife to be quite free. It did not occur to him that he had done anything extraordinary, either in deserting his wife or in forwarding false news of his death. He had done the simple thing, the casual thing, the blunt thing, the thing that necessitated the minimum of talking. He did not intend to return to England.

However, after a few years, he did return to England. The cause of his return is irrelevant to the history, but I may say that it sprang from a conflict between the Five Towns temperament and the Trenton Union of Earthenware Operatives. Such is the power of Unions in the United States that Toby, if he wished to remain under the Federal Flag, had either to yield or to starve. He would not yield. He changed his name and came to England; strolled calmly into the Crown Porcelain Works at Derby one day, and there recommenced his career as an artificer of earthenware. He did well. He could easily earn four pounds a week, and had no desires, save in the direction of fly-fishing—not an expensive diversion. He knew better than to marry. He existed quietly; and one year trod on the heels of another, and carried him from thirty to forty and forty to fifty, and no one found out his identity, though there are several direct trains daily between Derby and Knype.

And now, owing to the death of a friend and a glass of beer, he was in Child Row, crossing the street towards the house whose ownership had caused him to quit it.

He knocked on the door with the handle of his umbrella. There was no knocker; there never had been a knocker. III

The door opened cautiously, as such doors in the Five Towns do, after a shooting of bolts and a loosing of chains; it opened to the extent of about nine inches, and Toby Hall saw the face of a middle-aged woman eyeing him.

'Is this Mrs Hall's?' he asked sternly.

'No. It ain't Mrs Hall's. It's Mrs Tansley's.'

'I thowt—'

The door opened a little wider.

'That's not you, Tobias?' said the woman unmoved.

'I reckon it is, though,' replied Toby, with a difficult smile.

'Bless us!' exclaimed the woman. The door oscillated slightly under her hand. 'Bless us!' she repeated. And then suddenly, 'You'd happen better come in, Tobias.'

'Aye!' said Tobias.

And he entered.

'Sit ye down, do,' said his wife. 'I thowt as you were dead. They wrote and told me so.'

'Aye!' said Tobias. 'But I am na'.'

He sat down in an arm-chair near the old-fashioned grate, with its hobs at either side. He was acquainted with that chair, and it had not appreciably altered since his departure. The lastingness of furniture under fair treatment is astonishing. This chair was uncomfortably in exactly the same spot where it had always been uncomfortable; and the same anti-macassar was draped over its uncompromising back. Toby put his hat on the table, and leaned his umbrella against the chimney-piece. His overcoat he retained. Same table; same chimney-piece; same clock and ornaments on the chimney-piece! But a different carpet on the floor, and different curtains before the window.

Priscilla bolted and chained the door, and then she too sat down. Her gown was black, with a small black silk apron. And she was stout, and she wore felt slippers and moved with the same gingerly care as Toby himself did. She looked fully her years. Her thin lips were firmer than ever. It was indeed Priscilla.

'Well, well!' she murmured.

But her capacity for wonder was nearly exhausted.

'Aye!' said Toby, with an air that was meant to be quasi-humorous. He warmed his hands at the fire, and then rubbed them over the front of his calves, leaning forward.

'So ye've come back?' said Priscilla.

'Aye!' concurred Toby.

There was a pause.

'Cold weather we're having,' he muttered.

'It's seasonable,' Priscilla pointed out.

Her glance rested on a sprig of holly that was tied under the gas- chandelier, unique relic of Christmas in the apartment.

Another pause. It would be hazardous to guess what their feelings were; perhaps their feelings were scarcely anything at all.

'And what be the news?' Toby inquired, with what passes in the Five Towns for geniality.

'News?' she repeated, as if not immediately grasping the significance of the question. 'I don't know as there's any news, nothing partic'ler, that is.'

Hung on the wall near the chimney-piece was a photograph of a girl. It was an excellent likeness to Priscilla, as she was in Toby's pre-Trenton days. How young and fresh the creature looked; so simple, so inexperienced! It startled Toby.

'I don't remember that,' he said.

'What?'

'That!' And he jerked his elbow towards the photograph.

'Oh! THAT! That's my daughter,' said Priscilla.

'Bless us!' said Toby in turn.

'I married Job Tansley,' Priscilla continued. 'He died four years ago last Knype Wakes Monday. HER'S married'—indicating the photograph—'her married young Gibson last September.'

'Well, well!' murmured Toby.

Another pause.

There was a shuffling on the pavement outside, and some children began to sing about shepherds and flocks.

'Oh, bother them childer,' said Priscilla. 'I must send 'em off.'

She got up.

'Here! Give 'em a penny,' Toby suggested, holding out a penny.

'Yes, and then they'll tell others, and I shan't have a moment's peace all night!' Priscilla grumbled.

However, she bestowed the penny, cutting the song off abruptly in the middle. And she bolted and chained the door and sat down again.

Another pause.

'Well, well!' said Priscilla.

'Aye!' Toby agreed. 'Good coal that!'

'Fourteen shilling a ton!'

Another pause, and a longer.

'Is Ned Walklate still at th' Rose and Crown?' Toby asked.

'For aught I know he is,' said Priscilla.

'I'll just step round there,' said Toby, picking up his hat and rising.

As he was manoeuvring the door-chain, Priscilla said—

'You're forgetting your umbrella, Tobias.'

'No,' he answered. 'I hanna' forgotten it. I'm coming back.'

Their eyes met, charged with meaning.

'That'll be all right,' she said. 'Well, well!'

'Aye!'

And he stepped round to Ned Walklate's.

FROM ONE GENERATION TO ANOTHER

I

It is the greatest mistake in the world to imagine that, because the Five Towns is an industrial district, devoted to the manufacture of cups and saucers, marbles and door-knobs, therefore there is no luxury in it.

A writer, not yet deceased, who spent two nights there, and wrote four hundred pages about it, has committed herself to the assertion that there are no private carriages in its streets— only perambulators and tramcars.

That writer's reputation is ruined in the Five Towns. For the Five Towns, although continually complaining of bad times, is immensely wealthy, as well as immensely poor—a country of contrasts, indeed—and private carriages, if they do not abound, exist at any rate in sufficient numbers.

Nay, more, automobiles of the most expensive French and English makes fly dashingly along its hilly roads and scatter in profusion the rich black mud thereof.

On a Saturday afternoon in last spring, such an automobile stood outside the garden entrance of Bleakridge House, just halfway between Hanbridge and Bursley. It belonged to young Harold Etches, of Etches, Limited, the great porcelain manufacturers.

It was a 20 h.p. Panhard, and was worth over a thousand pounds as it stood there, throbbing, and Harold was proud of it.

He was also proud of his young wife, Maud, who, clad in several hundred pounds' worth of furs, had taken her seat next to the steering-wheel, and was waiting for Harold to mount by her side. The united ages of this handsome and gay couple came to less than forty-five.

And they owned the motor-car, and Bleakridge House with its ten bedrooms, and another house at Llandudno, and a controlling interest in Etches, Limited, that brought them in seven or eight thousand a year. They were a pretty tidy example of what the Five Towns can do when it tries to be wealthy.

At that moment, when Harold was climbing into the car, a shabby old man who was walking down the road, followed by a boy carrying a carpet-bag, stopped suddenly and touched Harold on the shoulder.

'Bless us!' exclaimed the old man. And the boy and the carpet-bag halted behind him.

'What? Uncle Dan?' said Harold.

'Uncle Dan!' cried Maud, springing up with an enchanting smile. 'Why, it's ages since—'

'And what d'ye reckon ye'n gotten here?' demanded the old man.

'It's my new car,' Harold explained.

'And ca'st drive it, lad?' asked the old man.

'I should think I could!' said Harold confidently.

'H'm!' commented the old man, and then he shook hands, and thoroughly scrutinized Maud.

Now, this is the sort of thing that can only be seen and appreciated in a district like the Five Towns, where families spring into splendour out of nothing in the course of a couple of generations, and as often as not sink back again into nothing in the course of two generations more.

The Etches family is among the best known and the widest spread in the Five Towns. It originated in three brothers, of whom Daniel was the youngest. Daniel never married; the other two did. Daniel was not very fond of money; the other two were, and they founded the glorious firm of Etches. Harold was the grandson of one brother, and Maud was the Granddaughter of the other. Consequently, they both stood in the same relation to Dan, who was their great-uncle—addressed as uncle 'for short'.

There is a good deal of snobbery in the Five Towns, but it does not exist between relatives. The relatives in danger of suffering by it would never stand it. Besides, although Dan's income did not exceed two hundred a year, he was really richer than his grandnephew, since Dan lived on half his income, whereas Harold, aided by Maud, lived on all of his.

Consequently, despite the vast difference in their stations, clothes, and manners, Daniel and his young relatives met as equals. It would have been amusing to see anyone—even the Countess of Chell, who patronized the entire district—attempt to patronize Dan.

In his time he had been the greatest pigeon-fancier in the country.

'So you're paying a visit to Bursley, uncle?' said Maud.

'Aye!' Dan replied. 'I'm back i' owd Bosley. Sarah—my housekeeper, thou know'st—'

'Not dead?'

'No. Her inna' dead; but her sister's dead, and I've give her a week's play [holiday], and come away. Rat Edge'll see nowt o' me this side Easter.'

Rat Edge was the name of the village, five miles off, which Dan had honoured in his declining years.

'And where are you going to now?' asked Harold.

'I'm going to owd Sam Shawn's, by th' owd church, to beg a bed.'

'But you'll stop with us, of course?' said Harold.

'Nay, lad,' said Dan.

'Oh yes, uncle,' Maud insisted.

'Nay, lass,' said Dan.

'Indeed, you will, uncle,' said Maud positively. 'If you don't, I'll never speak to you again.'

She had a charming fire in her eyes, had Maud.

Daniel, the old bachelor, yielded at once, but in his own style.

'I'll try it for a night, lass,' said he.

Thus it occurred that the carpet-bag was carried into Bleakridge House, and that after some delay Harold and Maud carried off Uncle Dan with them in the car. He sat in the luxurious tonneau behind, and Maud had quitted her husband in order to join him. Possibly she liked the humorous wrinkles round his grey eyes.

Or it may have been the eyes themselves. And yet Dan was nearer seventy than sixty.

The car passed everything on the road; it seemed to be overtaking electric trams all the time.

'So ye'n been married a year?' said Uncle Dan, smiling at Maud.

'Oh yes; a year and three days. We're quite used to it.'

'Us'n be in h-ll in a minute, wench!' exclaimed Dan, calmly changing the topic, as Harold swung the car within an inch of a brewer's dray, and skidded slightly in the process. No anti- skidding device would operate in that generous, oozy mud.

And, as a matter of fact, they were in Hanbridge the next minute—Hanbridge, the centre of the religions, the pleasures, and the vices of the Five Towns.

'Bless us!' said the old man. 'It's fifteen year and more since I were here.'

'Harold,' said Maud, 'let's stop at the Piccadilly Cafe and have some tea.'

'Cafe?' asked Dan. 'What be that?'

'It's a kind of a pub.' Harold threw the explanation over his shoulder as he brought the car up with swift dexterity in front of the Misses Callear's newly opened afternoon tea-rooms.

'Oh, well, if it's a pub,' said Uncle Dan, 'I dunna' object.'

He frankly admitted, on entering, that he had never before seen a pub full of little tables and white cloths, and flowers, and young women, and silver teapots, and cake-stands. And though he did pour his tea into his saucer, he was sufficiently at home there to address the younger Miss Callear as 'young woman', and to inform her that her beverage was lacking in Orange Pekoe. And the Misses Callear, who conferred a favour on their customers in serving them, didn't like it.

He became reminiscent.

'Aye!' he said, 'when I left th' Five Towns fifty-two years sin' to go weaving i' Derbyshire wi' my mother's brother, tay were ten shilling a pun'. Us had it when us were sick—which wasna' often. We worked too hard for be sick. Hafe past five i' th' morning till eight of a night, and then Saturday afternoon walk ten mile to Glossop with a week's work on ye' back, and home again wi' th' brass.

'They've lost th' habit of work now-a-days, seemingly,' he went on, as the car moved off once more, but slowly, because of the vast crowds emerging from the Knype football ground. 'It's football, Saturday; bands of a Sunday; football, Monday; ill i' bed and getting round, Tuesday; do a bit o' work Wednesday; football, Thursday; draw wages Friday night; and football, Saturday. And wages higher than ever. It's that as beats me— wages higher than ever—

'Ye canna' smoke with any comfort i' these cars,' he added, when Harold had got clear of the crowds and was letting out. He regretfully put his pipe in his pocket.

Harold skirted the whole length of the Five Towns from south to north, at an average rate of perhaps thirty miles an hour; and quite soon the party found itself on the outer side of Turnhill, and descending the terrible Clough Bank, three miles long, and of a steepness resembling the steepness of the side of a house.

The car had warmed to its business, and Harold took them down that declivity in a manner which startled even Maud, who long ago had resigned herself to the fact that she was tied for life to a young man for whom the word 'danger' had no meaning.

At the bottom they had a swerve skid; but as there was plenty of room for eccentricities, nothing happened except that the car tried to climb the hill again.

'Well, if I'd known,' observed Uncle Dan, 'if I'd guessed as you were reservin' this treat for th' owd uncle, I'd ha' walked.'

The Etches blood in him was pretty cool, but his nerve had had a shaking.

Then Harold could not restart the car. The engine had stopped of its own accord, and, though Harold lavished much physical force on the magic handle in front, nothing would budge. Maud and the old man got down, the latter with relief.

'Stuck, eh?' said Dan. 'No steam?'

'That's it!' Harold cried, slapping his leg. 'What an ass I am! She wants petrol, that's all. Maud, pass a couple of cans. They're under the seat there, behind. No; on the left, child.'

However, there was no petrol on the car.

'That's that cursed Durand' (Durand being the new chauffeur— French, to match the car). 'I told him not to forget. Last thing I said to the fool! Maud, I shall chuck that chap!'

'Can't we do anything?' asked Maud stiffly, putting her lips together.

'We can walk back to Turnhill and buy some petrol, some of us!' snapped Harold. 'That's what we can do!'

'Sithee,' said Uncle Dan. 'There's the Plume o' Feathers half-a- mile back. Th' landlord's a friend o' mine. I can borrow his mare and trap, and drive to Turnhill and fetch some o' thy petrol, as thou calls it.'

'It's awfully good of you, uncle.'

'Nay, lad, I'm doing it for please mysen. But Maud mun come wi' me. Give us th' money for th' petrol, as thou calls it.'

'Then I must stay here alone?' Harold complained.

'Seemingly,' the old man agreed.

After a few words on pigeons, and a glass of beer, Dan had no difficulty whatever in borrowing his friend's white mare and black trap. He himself helped in the harnessing. Just as he was driving triumphantly away, with that delicious vision Maud on his left hand and a stable-boy behind, he reined the mare in.

'Give us a couple o' penny smokes, matey,' he said to the landlord, and lit one.

The mare could go, and Dan could make her go, and she did go. And the whole turn-out looked extremely dashing when, ultimately, it dashed into the glare of the acetylene lamps which the deserted Harold had lighted on his car.

The red end of a penny smoke in the gloom of twilight looks exactly as well as the red end of an Havana. Moreover, the mare caracolled ornamentally in the rays of the acetylene, and the stable-boy had to skip down quick and hold her head.

'How much didst say this traction-engine had cost thee?' Dan asked, while Harold was pouring the indispensable fluid into the tank.

'Not far off twelve hundred,' answered Harold lightly. 'Keep that cigar away from here.'

'Fifteen pun' ud buy this mare,' Dan announced to the road.

'Now, all aboard!' Harold commanded at length. 'How much shall I give to the boy for the horse and trap, uncle?'

'Nothing,' said Dan. 'I havena' finished wi' that mare yet. Didst think I was going to trust mysen i' that thing o' yours again? I'll meet thee at Bleakridge, lad.'

'And I think I'll go with uncle too, Harold,' said Maud.

Whereupon they both got into the trap.

Harold stared at them, astounded.

'But I say—' he protested, beginning to be angry.

Uncle Dan drove away like the wind, and the stable-boy had all he could do to clamber up behind.

II

Now, at dinner-time that night, in the dining-room of the commodious and well-appointed mansion of the youngest and richest of the Etches, Uncle Dan stood waiting and waiting for his host and hostess to appear. He was wearing a Turkish tasselled smoking- cap to cover his baldness, and he had taken off his jacket and put on his light, loose overcoat instead of it, since that was a comfortable habit of his.

He sent one of the two parlourmaids upstairs for his carpet slippers out of the carpet-bag, and he passed part of the time in changing his boots for his slippers in front of the fire. Then at length, just as a maid was staggering out under the load of those enormous boots, Harold appeared, very correct, but alone.

'Awfully sorry to keep you waiting, uncle,' said Harold, 'but Maud isn't well. She isn't coming down tonight.'

'What's up wi' Maud?'

'Oh, goodness knows!' responded Harold gloomily. 'She's not well— that's all.'

'H'm!' said Dan. 'Well, let's peck a bit.'

So they sat down and began to peck a bit, aided by the two maids. Dan pecked with prodigious enthusiasm, but Harold was not in good pecking form. And as the dinner progressed, and Harold sent dish after dish up to his wife, and his wife returned dish after dish untouched, Harold's gloom communicated itself to the house in general.

One felt that if one had penetrated to the farthest corner of the farthest attic, a little parcel of spiritual gloom would have already arrived there. The sense of disaster was in the abode. The cook was prophesying like anything in the kitchen. Durand in the garage was meditating upon such of his master's pithy remarks as he had been able to understand.

When the dinner was over, and the coffee and liqueurs and cigars had been served, and the two maids had left the dining-room, Dan turned to his grandnephew and said—

'There's things as has changed since my time, lad, but human nature inna' one on em.'

'What do you mean, uncle?' Harold asked awkwardly, self- consciously.

'I mean as thou'rt a dashed foo'!'

'Why?'

'But thou'lt get better o' that,' said Dan.

Harold smiled sheepishly.

'I don't know what you're driving at, uncle,' said he.

'Yes, thou dost, lad. Thou'st been and quarrelled wi' Maud. And I say thou'rt a dashed foo'!'

'As a matter of fact—' Harold stammered.

'And ye've never quarrelled afore. This is th' fust time. And so thou'st under th' impression that th' world's come to an end. Well, th' fust quarrel were bound to come sooner or later.'

'It isn't really a quarrel—it's about nothing—'

'I know—I know,' Dan broke in. 'They always are. As for it not being a quarrel, lad, call it a picnic if thou'st a mind. But heir's sulking upstairs, and thou'rt sulking down here.'

'She was cross about the petrol,' said Harold, glad to relieve his mind. 'I hadn't a notion she was cross till I went up into the bedroom. Not a notion! I explained to her it wasn't my fault. I argued it out with her very calmly. I did my best to reason with her—'

'Listen here, young 'un,' Dan interrupted him. 'How old art?'

'Twenty-three.'

'Thou may'st live another fifty years. If thou'st a mind to spend 'em i' peace, thoud'st better give up reasoning wi' women. Give it up right now! It's worse nor drink, as a habit. Kiss 'em, cuddle 'em, beat 'em. But dunna' reason wi' 'em.'

'What should you have done in my place?' Harold asked.

'I should ha' told Maud her was quite right.'

'But she wasn't.'

'Then I should ha' winked at mysen i' th' glass,' continued Dan, 'and kissed her.'

'That's all very well—'

'Naturally,' said Dan, 'her wanted to show off that car i' front o' me. That was but natural. And her was vexed when it went wrong.'

'But I told her—I explained to her.'

'Her's a handsome little wench,' Dan proceeded. 'And a good heart. But thou'st got ten times her brains, lad, and thou ought'st to ha' given in.'

'But I can't always be—'

'It's allus them as gives in as has their own way. I remember her grandfather—he was th' eldest o' us—he quarrelled wi' his wife afore they'd been married a week, and she raced him all over th' town wi' a besom—'

'With a besom, uncle?' exclaimed Harold, shocked at these family disclosures.

'Wi' a besom,' said Dan. That come o' reasoning wi' a woman. It taught him a lesson, I can tell thee. And afterwards he always said as nowt was worth a quarrel—NOWT! And it isna'.'

'I don't think Maud will race me all over the town with a besom,' Harold remarked reflectively.

'There's worse things nor that,' said Dan. 'Look thee here, get out o' th' house for a' 'our. Go to th' Conservative Club, and then come back. Dost understand?'

'But what—'

'Hook it, lad!' said Dan curtly.

And just as Harold was leaving the room, like a school-boy, he called him in again.

'I havena' told thee, Harold, as I'm subject to attacks. I'm getting up in years. I go off like. It isna' fits, but I go off. And if it should happen while I'm here, dunna' be alarmed.'

'What are we to do?'

'Do nothing. I come round in a minute or two. Whatever ye do, dunna' give me brandy. It might kill me—so th' doctor says. I'm only telling thee in case.'

'Well, I hope you won't have an attack,' said Harold.

'It's a hundred to one I dunna',' said Dan.

And Harold departed.

Soon afterwards Uncle Dan wandered into a kitchen full of servants.

'Show me th' missis's bedroom, one on ye,' he said to the crowd.

And presently he was knocking at Maud's door.

'Maudie!'

'Who is it?' came a voice.

'It's thy owd uncle. Can'st spare a minute?'

Maud appeared at the door, smiling, and arrayed in a peignoir.

'HE'S gone out,' said Dan, implying scorn of the person who had gone out. 'Wilt come down-stairs?'

'Where's he gone to?' Maud demanded.

She didn't even pretend she was ill.

'Th' Club,' said Dan.

And in about a hundred seconds or so he had her in the drawing- room, and she was actually pouring out gin for him. She looked ravishing in that peignoir, especially as she was munching an apple, and balancing herself on the arm of a chair.

'So he's been quarrelling with ye, Maud?' Dan began.

'No; not quarrelling, uncle.'

'Well, call it what ye'n a mind,' said Dan. 'Call it a prayer- meeting. I didn't notice as ye came down for supper—dinner, as ye call it.'

'It was like this, uncle,' she said. 'Poor Harry was very angry with himself about that petrol. Of course, he wanted the car to go well while you were in it; and he came up-stairs and grumbled at me for leaving him all alone and driving home with you.'

'Oh, did he?' exclaimed Dan.

'Yes. I explained to him that of course I couldn't leave you all alone. Then he got hot. I kept quite calm. I reasoned it out with him as quietly as I could—'

'Maudie, Maudie,' protested the old man, 'thou'rt th' prettiest wench i' this town, though I AM thy great-uncle, and thou'st got plenty o' brains—a sight more than that husband o' thine.'

'Do you think so, uncle?'

'Aye, but thou hasna' made use o' 'em tonight. Thou'rt a foolish wench, wench. At thy time o' life, and after a year o' th' married state, thou ought'st to know better than reason wi' a man in a temper.'

'But, really, uncle, it was so absurd of Harold, wasn't it?'

'Aye!' said Dan. 'But why didst-na' give in and kiss him, and smack his face for him?'

'There was nothing to give in about, uncle.'

'There never is,' said Dan. 'There never is. That's the point. Still, thou'rt nigh crying, wench.'

'I'm not, uncle,' she contradicted, the tears falling on to the apple.

'And Harold's using bad language all up Trafalgar Road, I lay,' Dan added.

'It was all Harold's fault,' said Maud.

'Why, in course it were Harold's fault. But nowt's worth a quarrel, my dear—NOWT. I remember Harold's grandfeyther—he were th' second of us, your grandfeyther were the eldest, and I were the youngest—I remember Harold's grandfeyther chasing his wife all over th' town wi' a besom a week after they were married.'

'With a besom!' murmured Maud, pained and forgetting to cry. 'Harold's grandfather, not mine?'

'Wi' a besom,' Dan repeated, nodding. 'They never quarrelled again—ne'er again. Th' old woman allus said after that as quarrels were for fools. And her was right.'

'I don't see Harold chasing me across Bursley with a besom,' said Maud primly. 'But what you say is quite right, you dear old uncle. Men are queer—I mean husbands. You can't argue with them. You'd much better give in—'

'And have your own way after all.'

'And perhaps Harold was—'

Harold's step could be heard in the hall.

'Oh, dear!' cried Maud. 'What shall I do?'

'I'm not feeling very well,' whispered Uncle Dan weakly. 'I have these 'ere attacks sometimes. There's only one thing as'll do me any good—brandy.'

And his head fell over one side of the chair, and he looked precisely like a corpse.

'Maud, what are you doing?' almost shouted Harold, when he came into the room.

She was putting a liqueur-glass to Uncle Dan's lips.

'Oh, Harold,' she cried, 'uncle's had an attack of some sort. I'm giving him some brandy.'

'But you mustn't give him brandy,' said Harold authoritatively to her.

'But I MUST give him brandy,' said Maud. 'He told me that brandy was the only thing to save him.'

'Nonsense, child!' Harold persisted. 'Uncle told ME all about these attacks. They're perfectly harmless so long as he doesn't have brandy. The doctors have warned him that brandy will be fatal.'

'Harold, you are absolutely mistaken. Don't you understand that uncle has only this minute told me that he MUST have brandy?'

And she again approached the glass to the pale lips of the old man. His tasselled Turkish smoking-cap had fallen to the floor, and the hemisphere of his bald head glittered under the gas.

'Maud, I forbid you!' And Harold put a hand on the glass. 'It's a matter of life and death. You must have misunderstood uncle.'

'It was you who misunderstood uncle,' said Maud. 'Of course, if you mean to prevent me by brute force—'

They both paused and glanced at Daniel, and then at each other.

'Perhaps you are right, dearest,' said Harold, in a new tone.

'No, dearest,' said Maud, also in a new tone. 'I expect you are right. I must have misunderstood.'

'No, no, Maud. Give him the brandy by all means. I've no doubt you're right.'

'But if you think I'd better not give it him—'

'But I would prefer you to give it him, dearest. It isn't likely you would be mistaken in a thing like that.'

'I would prefer to be guided by you, dearest,' said Maud.

So they went on for several minutes, each giving way to the other in the most angelic manner.

'AND MEANTIME I'M SUPPOSED TO BE DYING, AM I?' roared Uncle Dan, suddenly sitting up. 'You'd let th' old uncle peg out while you practise his precepts! A nice pair you make! I thought for see which on ye' ud' give way to th' other, but I didna' anticipate as both on ye 'ud be ready to sacrifice my life for th' sake o' domestic peace.'

'But, uncle,' they both said later, amid the universal and yet rather shamefaced peace rejoicings, 'you said nothing was worth a quarrel.'

'And I was right,' answered Dan; 'I was right. Th' Divorce Court is full o' fools as have begun married life by trying to convince the other fool, instead o' humouring him—or her. Kiss us, Maud.'

THE DEATH OF SIMON FUGE

It was in the train that I learnt of his death. Although a very greedy eater of literature, I can only enjoy reading when I have little time for reading. Give me three hours of absolute leisure, with nothing to do but read, and I instantly become almost incapable of the act. So it is always on railway journeys, and so it was that evening. I was in the middle of Wordsworth's Excursion; I positively gloated over it, wondering why I should have allowed a mere rumour that it was dull to prevent me from consuming it earlier in my life. But do you suppose I could continue with Wordsworth in the train? I could not. I stared out of the windows; I calculated the speed of the train by my watch; I thought of my future and my past; I drew forth my hopes, examined them, polished them, and put them back again; I forgave myself for my sins; and I dreamed of the exciting conquest of a beautiful and brilliant woman that I should one day achieve. In short, I did everything that men habitually do under such circumstances. The Gazette was lying folded on the seat beside me: one of the two London evening papers that a man of taste may peruse without humiliating himself. How appetizing a morsel, this sheet new and smooth from the press, this sheet written by an ironic, understanding, small band of men for just a few thousand persons like me, ruthlessly scornful of the big circulations and the idols of the people! If the Gazette and its sole rival ceased to appear, I do believe that my existence and many similar existences would wear a different colour. Could one dine alone in Jermyn Street or Panton Street without this fine piquant evening commentary on the gross newspapers of the morning? (Now you perceive what sort of a man I am, and you guess, rightly, that my age is between thirty and forty.) But the train had stopped at Rugby and started again, and more than half of my journey was accomplished, ere at length I picked up the Gazette, and opened it with the false calm of a drunkard who has sworn that he will not wet his lips before a certain hour. For, well knowing from experience that I should suffer acute ennui in the train, I had, when buying the Gazette at Euston, taken oath that I would not even glance at it till after Rugby; it is always the final hour of these railway journeys that is the nethermost hell.

The second thing that I saw in the Gazette (the first was of course the 'Entremets' column of wit, humour, and parody, very uneven in its excellence) was the death of Simon Fuge. There was nearly a column about it, signed with initials, and the subheading of the article ran, 'Sudden death of a great painter'. That was characteristic of the Gazette. That Simon Fuge was indeed a great painter is now admitted by most dilettantes, though denied by a few. But to the great public he was not one of the few great names. To the great public he was just a medium name. Ten to one that in speaking of him to a plain person you would feel compelled to add: 'The painter, you know,' and the plain person would respond: 'Oh yes,' falsely pretending that he was perfectly familiar with the name. Simon Fuge had many friends on the press, and it was solely owing to the loyalty of these friends in the matter of obituary notices that the great public heard more of Simon Fuge in the week after his death than it had heard of him during the thirty-five years of his life. It may be asked: Why, if he had so many and such loyal friends on the press, these friends did not take measures to establish his reputation before he died? The answer is that editors will not allow journalists to praise a living artist much in excess of the esteem in which the public holds him; they are timid. But when a misunderstood artist is dead the editors will put no limit on laudation. I am not on the press, but it happens that I know the world.

Of all the obituary notices of Simon Fuge, the Gazette's was the first. Somehow the Gazette had obtained exclusive news of the little event, and some one high up on the Gazette's staff had a very exalted notion indeed of Fuge, and must have known him personally. Fuge received his deserts as a painter in that column of print. He was compared to Sorolla y Bastida for vitality; the morbidezza of his flesh-tints was stated to be unrivalled even by —I forget the name, painting is not my speciality. The writer blandly inquired why examples of Fuge's work were to be seen in the Luxembourg, at Vienna, at Florence, at Dresden; and not, for instance, at the Tate Gallery, or in the Chantrey collection. The writer also inquired, with equal blandness, why a painter who had been on the hanging committee of the Societe Nationale des Beaux Arts at Paris should not have been found worthy to be even an A.R.A. in London. In brief, old England 'caught it', as occurred somewhere or other most nights in the columns of the Gazette. Fuge also received his deserts as a man. And the Gazette did not conceal that he had not been a man after the heart of the British public. He had been too romantically and intensely alive for that. The writer gave a little penportrait of him. It was very good, recalling his tricks of manner, his unforgettable eyes, and his amazing skill in talking about himself and really interesting everybody in himself. There was a special reference to one of Fuge's most dramatic recitals—a narration of a night spent in a boat on Ham Lake with two beautiful girls, sisters, natives of the Five Towns, where Fuge was born. Said the obituarist: 'Those two wonderful creatures who played so large a part in Simon Fuge's life.'

This death was a shock to me. It took away my ennui for the rest of the journey. I too had known Simon Fuge. That is to say, I had met him once, at a soiree, and on that single occasion, as luck had it, he had favoured the company with the very narration to which the Gazette contributor referred. I remembered well the burning brilliance of his blue-black eyes, his touching assurance that all of us were necessarily interested in his adventures, and the extremely graphic and convincing way in which he reconstituted for us the nocturnal scene on Ham Lake—the two sisters, the boat, the rustle of trees, the lights on shore, and his own difficulty in managing the oars, one of which he lost for half-an-hour and found again. It was by such details as that about the oar that, with a tint of humour, he added realism to the romantic quality of his tales. He seemed to have no reticences concerning himself. Decidedly he allowed things to be understood...! Yes, his was a romantic figure, the figure of one to whom every day, and every hour of the day, was coloured by the violence of his passion for existence. His pictures had often an unearthly beauty, but for him they were nothing but faithful renderings of what he saw.

My mind dwelt on those two beautiful sisters. Those two beautiful sisters appealed to me more than anything else in the Gazette's obituary. Surely—Simon Fuge had obviously been a man whose emotional susceptibility and virile impulsiveness must have opened the door for him to multifarious amours—but surely he had not made himself indispensable to both sisters simultaneously. Surely even he had not so far forgotten that Ham Lake was in the middle of a country called England, and not the ornamental water in the Bois de Boulogne! And yet.... The delicious possibility of ineffable indiscretions on the part of Simon Fuge monopolized my mind till the train stopped at Knype, and I descended. Nevertheless, I think I am a serious and fairly insular Englishman. It is truly astonishing how a serious person can be obsessed by trifles that, to speak mildly, do not merit sustained attention.

I wondered where Ham Lake was. I knew merely that it lay somewhere in the environs of the Five Towns. What put fuel on the fire of my interest in the private affairs of the dead painter was the slightly curious coincidence that on the evening of the news of his death I should be travelling to the Five Towns—and for the first time in my life. Here I was at Knype, which, as I had gathered from Bradshaw, and from my acquaintance Brindley, was the traffic centre of the Five Towns.

II

My knowledge of industrial districts amounted to nothing. Born in Devonshire, educated at Cambridge, and fulfilling my destiny as curator of a certain department of antiquities at the British Museum, I had never been brought into contact with the vast constructive material activities of Lancashire, Yorkshire, and Staffordshire. I had but passed through them occasionally on my way to Scotland, scorning their necessary grime with the perhaps too facile disdain of the clean-faced southerner, who is apt to forget that coal cannot walk up unaided out of the mine, and that the basin in which he washes his beautiful purity can only be manufactured amid conditions highly repellent. Well, my impressions of the platform of Knype station were unfavourable. There was dirt in the air; I could feel it at once on my skin. And the scene was shabby, undignified, and rude. I use the word 'rude' in all its senses. What I saw was a pushing, exclamatory, ill-dressed, determined crowd, each member of which was bent on the realization of his own desires by the least ceremonious means. If an item of this throng wished to get past me, he made me instantly aware of his wish by abruptly changing my position in infinite space; it was not possible to misconstrue his meaning. So much crude force and naked will-to-live I had not before set eyes on. In truth, I felt myself to be a very brittle, delicate bit of intellectual machinery in the midst of all these physical manifestations. Yet I am a tallish man, and these potters appeared to me to be undersized, and somewhat thin too! But what elbows! What glaring egoistic eyes! What terrible decisiveness in action!

'Now then, get in if ye're going!' said a red-haired porter to me curtly.

'I'm not going. I've just got out,' I replied.

'Well, then, why dunna' ye stand out o' th' wee and let them get in as wants to?'

Unable to offer a coherent answer to this crushing demand, I stood out of the way. In the light of further knowledge I now surmise that that porter was a very friendly and sociable porter. But at the moment I really believed that, taking me for the least admirable and necessary of God's creatures, he meant to convey his opinion to me for my own good. I glanced up at the lighted windows of the train, and saw the composed, careless faces of haughty persons who were going direct from London to Manchester, and to whom the Five Towns was nothing but a delay. I envied them. I wanted to return to the shelter of the train. When it left, I fancied that my last link with civilization was broken. Then another train puffed in, and it was simply taken by assault in a fraction of time, to an incomprehensible bawling of friendly sociable porters. Season-ticket holders at Finsbury Park think they know how to possess themselves of a train; they are deceived. So this is where Simon Fuge came from (I reflected)! The devil it is (I reflected)! I tried to conceive what the invaders of the train would exclaim if confronted by one of Simon Fuge's pictures. I could imagine only one word, and that a monosyllable, that would meet the case of their sentiments. And his dalliance, his tangential nocturnal deviations in gondolas with exquisite twin odalisques! There did not seem to be much room for amorous elegance in the lives of these invaders. And his death! What would they say of his death? Upon my soul, as I stood on that dirty platform, in a milieu of advertisements of soap, boots, and aperients, I began to believe that Simon Fuge never had lived, that he was a mere illusion of his friends and his small public. All that I saw around me was a violent negation of Simon Fuge, that entity of rare, fine, exotic sensibilities, that perfectly mad gourmet of sensations, that exotic seer of beauty.

I caught sight of my acquaintance and host, Mr Robert Brindley, coming towards me on the platform. Hitherto I had only met him in London, when, as chairman of the committee of management of the Wedgwood Institution and School of Art at Bursley, he had called on me at the British Museum for advice as to loan exhibits. He was then dressed like a self-respecting tourist. Now, although an architect by profession, he appeared to be anxious to be mistaken for a sporting squire. He wore very baggy knickerbockers, and leggings, and a cap. This raiment was apparently the agreed uniform of the easy classes in the Five Towns; for in the crowd I had noticed several such consciously superior figures among the artisans. Mr Brindley, like most of the people in the station, had a slightly pinched and chilled air, as though that morning he had by inadvertence omitted to don those garments which are not seen. He also, like most of the people there, but not to the same extent, had a somewhat suspicious and narrowly shrewd regard, as who should say: 'If any person thinks he can get the better of me by a trick, let him try—that's all.' But the moment his eye encountered mine, this expression vanished from his face, and he gave me a candid smile.

'I hope you're well,' he said gravely, squeezing my hand in a sort of vice that he carried at the end of his right arm.

I reassured him.

'Oh, I'm all right,' he said, in response to the expression of my hopes.

It was a relief to me to see him. He took charge of me. I felt, as it were, safe in his arms. I perceived that, unaided and unprotected, I should never have succeeded in reaching Bursley from Knype.

A whistle sounded.

'Better get in,' he suggested; and then in a tone of absolute command: 'Give me your bag.'

I obeyed. He opened the door of a first-class carriage.

'I'm travelling second,' I explained.

'Never mind. Get in.'

In his tones was a kindly exasperation.

I got in; he followed. The train moved.

'Ah!' breathed Mr Brindley, blowing out much air and falling like a sack of coal into a corner seat. He was a thin man, aged about thirty, with brown eyes, and a short blonde beard.

Conversation was at first difficult. Personally I am not a bubbling fount of gay nothings when I find myself alone with a comparative stranger. My drawbridge goes up as if by magic, my postern is closed, and I peer cautiously through the narrow slits of my turret to estimate the chances of peril. Nor was Mr Brindley offensively affable. However, we struggled into a kind of chatter. I had come to the Five Towns, on behalf of the British Museum, to inspect and appraise, with a view to purchase by the nation, some huge slip-decorated dishes, excessively curious according to photographs, which had been discovered in the cellars of the Conservative Club at Bursley. Having shared in the negotiations for my visit, Mr Brindley had invited me to spend the night at his house. We were able to talk about all this. And when we had talked about all this we were able to talk about the singular scenery of coal dust, potsherds, flame and steam, through which the train wound its way. It was squalid ugliness, but it was squalid ugliness on a scale so vast and overpowering that it became sublime. Great furnaces gleamed red in the twilight, and their fires were reflected in horrible black canals; processions of heavy vapour drifted in all directions across the sky, over what acres of mean and miserable brown architecture! The air was alive with the most extraordinary, weird, gigantic sounds. I do not think the Five Towns will ever be described: Dante lived too soon. As for the erratic and exquisite genius, Simon Fuge, and his odalisques reclining on silken cushions on the enchanted bosom of a lake—I could no longer conjure them up even faintly in my mind.

'I suppose you know Simon Fuge is dead?' I remarked, in a pause.

'No! Is he?' said Mr Brindley, with interest. 'Is it in the paper?'

He did not seem to be quite sure that it would be in the paper.

'Here it is,' said I, and I passed him the Gazette.

'Ha!' he exclaimed explosively. This 'Ha!' was entirely different from his 'Ah!' Something shot across his eyes, something incredibly rapid—too rapid for a wink; yet it could only be called a wink. It was the most subtle transmission of the beyond- speech that I have ever known any man accomplish, and it endeared Mr Brindley to me. But I knew not its significance.

'What do they think of Fuge down here?' I asked.

'I don't expect they think of him,' said my host.

He pulled a pouch and a packet of cigarette papers from his pocket.

'Have one of mine,' I suggested, hastily producing my case.

He did not even glance at its contents.

'No, thanks,' he said curtly.

I named my brand.

'My dear sir,' he said, with a return to his kindly exasperation, 'no cigarette that is not fresh made can be called a cigarette.' I stood corrected. 'You may pay as much as you like, but you can never buy cigarettes as good as I can make out of an ounce of fresh B.D.V. tobacco. Can you roll one?' I had to admit that I could not, I who in Bloomsbury was accepted as an authority on cigarettes as well as on porcelain. 'I'll roll you one, and you shall try it.'

He did so.

I gathered from his solemnity that cigarettes counted in the life of Mr Brindley. He could not take cigarettes other than seriously. The worst of it was that he was quite right. The cigarette which he constructed for me out of his wretched B.D.V. tobacco was adorable, and I have made my own cigarettes ever since. You will find B.D.V. tobacco all over the haunts frequented by us of the

Museum now-a-days, solely owing to the expertise of Mr Brindley. A terribly capable and positive man! He KNEW, and he knew that he knew.

He said nothing further as to Simon Fuge. Apparently he had forgotten the decease.

'Do you often see the Gazette?' I asked, perhaps in the hope of attracting him back to Fuge.

'No,' he said; 'the musical criticism is too rotten.'

Involuntarily I bridled. It was startling, and it was not agreeable, to have one's favourite organ so abruptly condemned by a provincial architect in knickerbockers and a cap, in the midst of all that industrial ugliness. What could the Five Towns know about art? Yet here was this fellow condemning the Gazette on artistic grounds. I offered no defence, because he was right— again. But I did not like it.

'Do you ever see the Manchester Guardian?' he questioned, carrying the war into my camp.

'No,' I said.

'Pity!' he ejaculated.

'I've often heard that it's a very good paper,' I said politely.

'It isn't a very good paper,' he laid me low. 'It's the best paper in the world. Try it for a month—it gets to Euston at half-past eight—and then tell me what you think.'

I saw that I must pull myself together. I had glided into the Five Towns in a mood of gentle, wise condescension. I saw that it would be as well, for my own honour and safety, to put on another mood as quickly as possible, otherwise I might be left for dead on the field. Certainly the fellow was provincial, curt, even brutal in his despisal of diplomacy. Certainly he exaggerated the importance of cigarettes in the great secular scheme of evolution. But he was a man; he was a very tonic dose. I thought it would be safer to assume that he knew everything, and that the British Museum knew very little. Yet at the British Museum he had been quite different, quite deferential and rather timid. Still, I liked him. I liked his eyes.

The train stopped at an incredible station situated in the centre of a rolling desert whose surface consisted of broken pots and cinders. I expect no one to believe this.

'Here we are,' said he blithely. 'No, give me the bag. Porter!'

His summons to the solitary porter was like a clap of thunder.

III

He lived in a low, blackish-crimson heavy-browed house at the corner of a street along which electric cars were continually thundering. There was a thin cream of mud on the pavements and about two inches of mud in the roadway, rich, nourishing mud like Indian ink half-mixed. The prospect of carrying a pound or so of that unique mud into a civilized house affrighted me, but Mr Brindley opened his door with his latchkey and entered the abode as unconcernedly as if some fair repentent had cleansed his feet with her tresses.

'Don't worry too much about the dirt,' he said. 'You're in Bursley.'

The house seemed much larger inside than out. A gas-jet burnt in the hall, and sombre portieres gave large mysterious hints of rooms. I could hear, in the distance, the noise of frizzling over a fire, and of a child crying. Then a tall, straight, wellmade, energetic woman appeared like a conjuring trick from behind a portiere.

'How do you do, Mr Loring?' she greeted me, smiling. 'So glad to meet you.'

'My wife,' Mr Brindley explained gravely.

'Now, I may as well tell you now, Bob,' said she, still smiling at me. 'Bobbie's got a sore throat and it may be mumps; the chimney's been on fire and we're going to be summoned; and you owe me sixpence.'

'Why do I owe you sixpence?'

'Because Annie's had her baby and it's a girl.'

'That's all right. Supper ready?'

'Supper is waiting for you.'

She laughed. 'Whenever I have anything to tell my husband, I always tell him at ONCE!' she said. 'No matter who's there.' She pronounced 'once' with a wholehearted enthusiasm for its vowel sound that I have never heard equalled elsewhere, and also with a very magnified 'w' at the beginning of it. Often when I hear the word 'once' pronounced in less downright parts of the world, I remember how they pronounce it in the Five Towns, and there rises up before me a complete picture of the district, its atmosphere, its spirit.

Mr Brindley led me to a large bathroom that had a faint odour of warm linen. In addition to a lot of assorted white babyclothes there were millions of towels in that bathroom. He turned on a tap and the place was instantly full of steam from a jet of boiling water.

'Now, then,' he said, 'you can start.'

As he showed no intention of leaving me, I did start. 'Mind you don't scald yourself,' he warned me, 'that water's HOT.' While I was washing, he prepared to wash. I suddenly felt as if I had been intimate with him and his wife for about ten years.

'So this is Bursley!' I murmured, taking my mouth out of a towel.

'Bosley, we call it,' he said. 'Do you know the limerick—"There was a young woman of Bosley"?'

'No.'

He intoned the local limerick. It was excellently good; not meet for a mixed company, but a genuine delight to the true amateur. One good limerick deserves another. It happened that I knew a number of the unprinted Rossetti limericks, precious things, not at all easy to get at. I detailed them to Mr Brindley, and I do not exaggerate when I say that I impressed him. I recovered all the ground I had lost upon cigarettes and newspapers. He appreciated those limericks with a juster taste than I should have expected. So, afterwards, did his friends. My belief is that I am to this day known and revered in Bursley, not as Loring the porcelain expert from the British Museum, but as the man who first, as it were, brought the good news of the Rossetti limericks from Ghent to Aix.

'Now, Bob,' an amicable voice shrieked femininely up from the ground-floor, 'am I to send the soup to the bathroom or are you coming down?'

A limerick will make a man forget even his dinner.

Mr Brindley performed once more with his eyes that something that was, not a wink, but a wink unutterably refined and spiritualized. This time I comprehended its import. Its import was to the effect that women are women.

We descended, Mr Brindley still in his knickerbockers.

'This way,' he said, drawing aside a portiere. Mrs Brindley, as we entered the room, was trotting a male infant round and round a table charged with everything digestible and indigestible. She handed the child, who was in its nightdress, to a maid.

'Say good night to father.'

'Good ni', faver,' the interesting creature piped.

'By-bye, sonny,' said the father, stooping to tickle. 'I suppose,' he added, when maid and infant had gone, 'if one's going to have mumps, they may as well all have it together.'

'Oh, of course,' the mother agreed cheerfully. 'I shall stick them all into a room.'

'How many children have you?' I inquired with polite curiosity.

'Three,' she said; 'that's the eldest that you've seen.'

What chiefly struck me about Mrs Brindley was her serene air of capableness, of having a self-confidence which experience had richly justified. I could see that she must be an extremely sensible mother. And yet she had quite another aspect too—how shall I explain it?—as though she had only had children in her spare time.

We sat down. The room was lighted by four candles, on the table. I am rather short-sighted, and so I did not immediately notice that there were low book-cases all round the walls. Why the presence of these book-cases should have caused me a certain astonishment I do not know, but it did. I thought of Knype station, and the scenery, and then the other little station, and the desert of pots and cinders, and the mud in the road and on the pavement and in the hall, and the baby-linen in the bathroom, and three children all down with mumps, and Mr Brindley's cap and knickerbockers and cigarettes; and somehow the books—I soon saw there were at least a thousand of them, and not circulating-library books, either, but BOOKS—well, they administered a little shock to me.

To Mr Brindley's right hand was a bottle of Bass and a corkscrew.

'Beer!' he exclaimed, with solemn ecstasy, with an ecstasy gross and luscious. And, drawing the cork, he poured out a glass, with fine skill in the management of froth, and pushed it towards me.

'No, thanks,' I said.

'No beer!' he murmured, with benevolent, puzzled disdain. 'Whisky?'

'No, thanks,' I said. 'Water.'

'*I* know what Mr Loring would like,' said Mrs Brindley, jumping up. 'I KNOW what Mr Loring would like.' She opened a cupboard and came back to the table with a bottle, which she planted in front of me. 'Wouldn't you, Mr Loring?'

It was a bottle of mercurey, a wine which has given me many dreadful dawns, but which I have never known how to refuse.

'I should,' I admitted; 'but it's very bad for me.'

'Nonsense!' said she. She looked at her husband in triumph.

'Beer!' repeated Mr Brindley with undiminished ecstasy, and drank about two-thirds of a glass at one try. Then he wiped the froth from his moustache. 'Ah!' he breathed low and soft. 'Beer!'

They called the meal supper. The term is inadequate. No term that I can think of would be adequate. Of its kind the thing was perfect. Mrs Brindley knew that it was perfect. Mr Brindley also knew that it was perfect. There were prawns in aspic. I don't know why I should single out that dish, except that it seemed strange to me to have crossed the desert of pots and cinders in order to encounter prawns in aspic. Mr Brindley ate more cold roast beef than I had ever seen any man eat before, and more pickled walnuts. It is true that the cold roast beef transcended all the cold roast beef of my experience. Mrs Brindley regaled herself largely on trifle, which Mr Brindley would not approach, preferring a most glorious Stilton cheese. I lost touch, temporarily, with the intellectual life. It was Mr Brindley who recalled me to it.

'Jane,' he said. (This was at the beef and pickles stage.)

No answer.

'Jane!'

Mrs Brindley turned to me. 'My name is not Jane,' she said, laughing, and making a moue simultaneously. 'He only calls me that to annoy me. I told him I wouldn't answer to it, and I won't. He thinks I shall give in because we've got "company"! But I won't treat you as "company", Mr Loring, and I shall expect you to take my side. What dreadful weather we're having, aren't we?'

'Dreadful!' I joined in the game.

'Jane!'

'Did you have a comfortable journey down?'

'Yes, thank you.'

'Well, then, Mary!' Mr Brindley yielded.

'Thank you very much, Mr Loring, for your kind assistance,' said his wife. 'Yes, dearest?'

Mr Brindley glanced at me over his second glass of beer.

'If those confounded kids are going to have mumps,' he addressed his words apparently into the interior of the glass, 'it probably means the doctor, and the doctor means money, and I shan't be able to afford the Hortulus Animoe.'

I opened my ears.

'My husband goes stark staring mad sometimes,' said Mrs Brindley to me. 'It lasts for a week or so, and pretty nearly lands us in the workhouse. This time it's the Hortulus Animoe. Do you know what it is? I don't.'

'No,' I said, and the prestige of the British Museum trembled. Then I had a vague recollection. 'There's an illuminated manuscript of that name in the Imperial Library of Vienna, isn't there?'

'You've got it in one,' said Mr Brindley. 'Wife, pass those walnuts.'

'You aren't by any chance buying it?' I laughed.

'No,' he said. 'A Johnny at Utrecht is issuing a facsimile of it, with all the hundred odd miniatures in colour. It will be the finest thing in reproduction ever done. Only seventy-five copies for England.'

'How much?' I asked.

'Well,' said he, with a preliminary look at his wife,'thirty-three pounds.'

'Thirty-three POUNDS!' she screamed. 'You never told me.'

'My wife never will understand,' said Mr Brindley, 'that complete confidence between two human beings is impossible.'

'I shall go out as a milliner, that's all,' Mrs Brindley returned. 'Remember, the Dictionary of National Biography isn't paid for yet.'

'I'm glad I forgot that, otherwise I shouldn't have ordered the Hortulus.'

'You've not ORDERED it?'

'Yes, I have. It'll be here tomorrow—at least the first part will.'

Mrs Brindley affected to fall back dying in her chair.

'Quite mad!' she complained to me. 'Quite mad. It's a hopeless case.'

But obviously she was very proud of the incurable lunatic.

'But you're a book-collector!' I exclaimed, so struck by these feats of extravagance in a modest house that I did not conceal my amazement.

'Did you think I collected postage-stamps?' the husband retorted. 'No, *I*'m not a book-collector, but our doctor is. He has a few books, if you like. Still, I wouldn't swop him; he's much too fond of fashionable novels.'

'You know you're always up his place,' said the wife; 'and I wonder what *I* should do if it wasn't for the doctor's novels!' The doctor was evidently a favourite of hers.

'I'm not always up at his place,' the husband contradicted. 'You know perfectly well I never go there before midnight. And HE knows perfectly well that I only go because he has the best whisky in the town. By the way, I wonder whether he knows that Simon Fuge is dead. He's got one of his etchings. I'll go up.'

'Who's Simon Fuge?' asked Mrs Brindley.

'Don't you remember old Fuge that kept the Blue Bell at Cauldon?'

'What? Simple Simon?'

'Yes. Well, his son.'

'Oh! I remember. He ran away from home once, didn't he, and his mother had a port-wine stain on her left cheek? Oh, of course. I remember him perfectly. He came down to the Five Towns some years ago for his aunt's funeral. So he's dead. Who told you?'

'Mr Loring.'

'Did you know him?' she glanced at me.

'I scarcely knew him,' said I. 'I saw it in the paper.'

'What, the Signal?'

'The Signal's the local rag,' Mr Brindley interpolated. 'No. It's in the Gazette.'

'The Birmingham Gazette?'

'No, bright creature—the Gazette,' said Mr Brindley.

'Oh!' She seemed puzzled.

'Didn't you know he was a painter?' the husband condescendingly catechized.

'I knew he used to teach at the Hanbridge School of Art,' said Mrs Brindley stoutly. 'Mother wouldn't let me go there because of that. Then he got the sack.'

'Poor defenceless thing! How old were you?'

'Seventeen, I expect.'

'I'm much obliged to your mother.'

'Where did he die?' Mrs Brindley demanded.

'At San Remo,' I answered. 'Seems queer him dying at San Remo in September, doesn't it?'

'Why?'

'San Remo is a winter place. No one ever goes there before December.'

'Oh, is it?' the lady murmured negligently. 'Then that would be just like Simon Fuge. *I* was never afraid of him,' she added, in a defiant tone, and with a delicious inconsequence that choked her husband in the midst of a draught of beer.

'You can laugh,' she said sturdily.

At that moment there was heard a series of loud explosive sounds in the street. They continued for a few seconds apparently just outside the dining-room window. Then they stopped, and the noise of the bumping electric cars resumed its sway over the ear.

'That's Oliver!' said Mr Brindley, looking at his watch. 'He must have come from Manchester in an hour and a half. He's a terror.'

'Glass! Quick!' Mrs Brindley exclaimed. She sprang to the sideboard, and seized a tumbler, which Mr Brindley filled from a second bottle of Bass. When the door of the room opened she was standing close to it, laughing, with the full, frothing glass in her hand.

A tall, thin man, rather younger than Mr Brindley and his wife, entered. He wore a long dust-coat and leggings, and he carried a motorist's cap in a great hand. No one spoke; but little puffs of laughter escaped all Mrs Brindley's efforts to imprison her mirth. Then the visitor took the glass with a magnificent broad smile, and said, in a rich and heavy Midland voice—

'Here's to moy wife's husband!'

And drained the nectar.

'Feel better now, don't you?' Mrs Brindley inquired.

'Aye, Mrs Bob, I do!' was the reply. 'How do, Bob?'

'How do?' responded my host laconically. And then with gravity: 'Mr Loring—Mr Oliver Colclough—thinks he knows something about music.'

'Glad to meet you, sir,' said Mr Colclough, shaking hands with me. He had a most attractively candid smile, but he was so long and lanky that he seemed to pervade the room like an omnipresence.

'Sit down and have a bit of cheese, Oliver,' said Mrs Brindley, as she herself sat down.

'No, thanks, Mrs Bob. I must be getting towards home.'

He leaned on her chair.

'Trifle, then?'

'No, thanks.'

'Machine going all right?'

'Like oil. Never stopped th' engine once.'

'Did you get the Sinfonia Domestica, Ol?' Mr Brindley inquired.

'Didn't I say as I should get it, Bob?'

'You SAID you would.'

'Well, I've got it.'

'In Manchester?'

'Of course.'

Mr Brindley's face shone with desire and Mr Oliver Colclough's face shone with triumph.

'Where is it?'

'In the hall.'

'My hall?'

'Aye!'

'We'll play it, Ol.'

'No, really, Bob! I can't stop now. I promised the wife—'

'We'll PLAY it, Ol! You'd no business to make promises. Besides, suppose you'd had a puncture!'

'I expect you've heard Strauss's Sinfonia Domestica, Mr Loring, up in the village?' Mr Colclough addressed me. He had surrendered to the stronger will.

'In London?' I said. 'No. But I've heard of it.'

'Bob and I heard it in Manchester last week, and we thought it 'ud be a bit of a lark to buy the arrangement for pianoforte duet.'

'Come and listen to it,' said Mr Brindley. 'That is, if nobody wants any more beer.'

IV

The drawing-room was about twice as large as the dining-room, and it contained about four times as much furniture. Once again there were books all round the walls. A grand piano, covered with music, stood in a corner, and behind was a cabinet full of bound music.

Mr Brindley, seated on one corner of the bench in front of the piano, cut the leaves of the Sinfonia Domestica.

'It's the devil!' he observed.

'Aye, lad!' agreed Mr Colclough, standing over him. 'It's difficult.'

'Come on,' said Mr. Brindley, when he had finished cutting.

'Better take your dust-coat off, hadn't you?' Mrs Brindley suggested to the friend. She and I were side by side on a sofa at the other end of the room.

'I may as well,' Mr Colclough admitted, and threw the long garment on to a chair. 'Look here, Bob, my hands are stiff with steering.'

'Don't find fault with your tools,' said Mr Brindley; 'and sit down. No, my boy, I'm going to play the top part. Shove along.'

'I want to play the top part because it's easiest,' Mr Colclough grumbled.

'How often have I told you the top part is never easiest? Who do you suppose is going to keep this symphony together—you or me?'

'Sorry I spoke.'

They arranged themselves on the bench, and Mr Brindley turned up the lower corners of every alternate leaf of the music.

'Now,' said he. 'Ready?'

'Let her zip,' said Mr Colclough.

They began to play. And then the door opened, and a servant, whose white apron was starched as stiff as cardboard, came in carrying a tray of coffee and unholy liqueurs, which she deposited with a rattle on a small table near the hostess.

'Curse!' muttered Mr Brindley, and stopped.

'Life's very complex, ain't it, Bob?' Mr Colclough murmured.

'Aye, lad.' The host glanced round to make sure that the rattling servant had entirely gone. 'Now start again.'

'Wait a minute, wait a minute!' cried Mrs Brindley excitedly. 'I'm just pouring out Mr Loring's coffee. There!' As she handed me the cup she whispered, 'We daren't talk. It's more than our place is worth.'

The performance of the symphony proceeded. To me, who am not a performer, it sounded excessively brilliant and incomprehensible. Mr Colclough stretched his right hand to turn over the page, and fumbled it. Another stoppage.

'Damn you, Ol!' Mr Brindley exploded. 'I wish you wouldn't make yourself so confoundedly busy. Leave the turning to me. It takes a great artist to turn over, and you're only a blooming chauffeur. We'll begin again.'

'Sackcloth!' Mr Colclough whispered.

I could not estimate the length of the symphony; but my impression was one of extreme length. Halfway through it the players both took their coats off. There was no other surcease.

'What dost think of it, Bob?' asked Mr Colclough in the weird silence that reigned after they had finished. They were standing up and putting on their coats and wiping their faces.

'I think what I thought before,' said Mr Brindley. 'It's childish.'

'It isn't childish,' the other protested. 'It's ugly, but it isn't childish.'

'It's childishly clever,' Mr Brindley modified his description. He did not ask my opinion.

'Coffee's cold,' said Mrs Brindley.

'I don't want any coffee. Give me some Chartreuse, please. Have a drop o' green, Ol?'

'A split soda 'ud be more in my line. Besides, I'm just going to have my supper. Never mind, I'll have a drop, missis, and chance it. I've never tried Chartreuse as an appetizer.'

At this point commenced a sanguinary conflict of wills to settle whether or not I also should indulge in green Chartreuse. I was defeated. Besides the Chartreuse, I accepted a cigar. Never before or since have I been such a buck.

'I must hook it,' said Mr Colclough, picking up his dust-coat.

'Not yet you don't,' said Mr Brindley. 'I've got to get the taste of that infernal Strauss out of my mouth. We'll play the first movement of the G minor? La-la-la—la-la-la—la-la-la-ta.' He whistled a phrase.

Mr Colclough obediently sat down again to the piano.

The Mozart was like an idyll after a farcical melodrama. They played it with an astounding delicacy. Through the latter half of the movement I could hear Mr Brindley breathing regularly and heavily through his nose, exactly as though he were being hypnotized. I had a tickling sensation in the small of my back, a sure sign of emotion in me. The atmosphere was changed.

'What a heavenly thing!' I exclaimed enthusiastically, when they had finished.

Mr Brindley looked at me sharply, and just nodded in silence. Well, good night, Ol.'

'I say,' said Mr Colclough; 'if you've nothing doing later on, bring Mr Loring round to my place. Will you come, Mr Loring? Do! Us'll have a drink.'

These Five Towns people certainly had a simple, sincere way of offering hospitality that was quite irresistible. One could see that hospitality was among their chief and keenest pleasures.

We all went to the front door to see Mr Colclough depart homewards in his automobile. The two great acetylene head-lights sent long glaring shafts of light down the side street. Mr Colclough, throwing the score of the Sinfonia Domestica into the tonneau of the immense car, put on a pair of gloves and began to circulate round the machine, tapping here, screwing there, as chauffeurs will. Then he bent down in front to start the engine.

'By the way, Ol,' Mr Brindley shouted from the doorway, 'it seems Simon Fuge is dead.'

We could see the man's stooping form between the two head-lights. He turned his head towards the house.

'Who the dagger is Simon Fuge?' he inquired. 'There's about five thousand Fuges in th' Five Towns.'

'Oh! I thought you knew him.'

'I might, and I mightn't. It's not one o' them Fuge brothers saggar-makers at Longshaw, is it?'

'No, It's—'

Mr Colclough had succeeded in starting his engine, and the air was rent with gun-shots. He jumped lightly into the driver's seat.

'Well, see you later,' he cried, and was off, persuading the enormous beast under him to describe a semicircle in the narrow street backing, forcing forward, and backing again, to the accompaniment of the continuous fusillade. At length he got away, drew up within two feet of an electric tram that slid bumping down the main street, and vanished round the corner. A little ragged boy passed, crying, 'Signal, extra,' and Mr Brindley hailed him.

'What IS Mr Colclough?' I asked in the drawing-room.

'Manufacturer—sanitary ware,' said Mr Brindley. 'He's got one of the best businesses in Hanbridge. I wish I'd half his income. Never buys a book, you know.'

'He seems to play the piano very well.'

'Well, as to that, he doesn't what you may call PLAY, but he's the best sight-reader in this district, bar me. I never met his equal. When you come across any one who can read a thing like the Domestic Symphony right off and never miss his place, you might send me a telegram. Colclough's got a Steinway. Wish I had.'

Mrs Brindley had been looking through the Signal.

'I don't see anything about Simon Fuge here,' said she.

'Oh, nonsense!' said her husband. 'Buchanan's sure to have got something in about it. Let's look.'

He received the paper from his wife, but failed to discover in it a word concerning the death of Simon Fuge.

'Dashed if I don't ring Buchanan up and ask him what he means! Here's a paper with an absolute monopoly in the district, and brings in about five thousand a year clear to somebody, and it doesn't give the news! There never is anything but advertisements and sporting results in the blessed thing.'

He rushed to his telephone, which was in the hall. Or rather, he did not rush; he went extremely quickly, with aggressive footsteps that seemed to symbolize just retribution. We could hear him at the telephone.

'Hello! No. Yes. Is that you, Buchanan? Well, I want Mr Buchanan. Is that you, Buchanan? Yes, I'm all right. What in thunder do you mean by having nothing in tonight about Simon Fuge's death? Eh? Yes, the Gazette. Well, I suppose you aren't Scotch for nothing. Why the devil couldn't you stop in Scotland and edit papers there?' Then a laugh. 'I see. Yes. What did you think of those cigars? Oh! See you at the dinner. Ta-ta.' A final ring.

'The real truth is, he wanted some advice as to the tone of his obituary notice,' said Mr Brindley, coming back into the drawing- room. 'He's got it, seemingly. He says he's writing it now, for tomorrow. He didn't put in the mere news of the death, because it was exclusive to the Gazette, and he's been having some difficulty with the Gazette lately. As he says, tomorrow afternoon will be quite soon enough for the Five Towns. It isn't as if Simon Fuge was a cricket match. So now you see how the wheels go round, Mr Loring.'

He sat down to the piano and began to play softly the Castle motive from the Nibelung's Ring. He kept repeating it in different keys.

'What about the mumps, wife?' he asked Mrs Brindley, who had been out of the room and now returned.

'Oh! I don't think it is mumps,' she replied. 'They're all asleep.'

'Good!' he murmured, still playing the Castle motive.

'Talking of Simon Fuge,' I said determined to satisfy my curiosity, 'who WERE the two sisters?'

'What two sisters?'

'That he spent the night in the boat with, on Ilam Lake.'

'Was that in the Gazette? I didn't read all the article.'

He changed abruptly into the Sword motive, which he gave with a violent flourish, and then he left the piano. 'I do beg you not to wake my children,' said his wife.

'Your children must get used to my piano,' said he. 'Now, then, what about these two sisters?'

I pulled the Gazette from my pocket and handed it to him. He read aloud the passage describing the magic night on the lake.

'*I* don't know who they were,' he said. 'Probably something tasty from the Hanbridge Empire.'

We both observed a faint, amused smile on the face of Mrs Brindley, the smile of a woman who has suddenly discovered in her brain a piece of knowledge rare and piquant.

'I can guess who they were,' she said. 'In fact, I'm sure.'

'Who?'

'Annie Brett and—you know who.'

'What, down at the Tiger?'

'Certainly. Hush!' Mrs Brindley ran to the door and, opening it, listened. The faint, fretful cry of a child reached us. 'There! You've done it! I told you you would!'

She disappeared. Mr Brindley whistled.

'And who is Annie Brett?' I inquired.

'Look here,' said he, with a peculiar inflection. 'Would you like to see her?'

'I should,' I said with decision.

'Well, come on, then. We'll go down to the Tiger and have a drop of something.'

'And the other sister?' I asked.

'The other sister is Mrs Oliver Colclough,' he answered. 'Curious, ain't it?'

Again there was that swift, scarcely perceptible phenomenon in his eyes.

V

We stood at the corner of the side-street and the main road, and down the main road a vast, white rectangular cube of bright light came plunging—its head rising and dipping—at express speed, and with a formidable roar. Mr Brindley imperiously raised his stick; the extraordinary box of light stopped as if by a miracle, and we jumped into it, having splashed through mud, and it plunged off again—bump, bump, bump—into the town of Bursley. As Mr Brindley passed into the interior of the car, he said laconically to two men who were smoking on the platform—

'How do, Jim? How do, Jo?'

And they responded laconically—

'How do, Bob?'

'How do, Bob?'

We sat down. Mr Brindley pointed to the condition of the floor.

'Cheerful, isn't it?' he observed to me, shouting above the din of vibrating glass.

Our fellow-passengers were few and unromantic, perhaps halfa-dozen altogether on the long, shiny, yellow seats of the car, each apparently lost in gloomy reverie.

'It's the advertisements and notices in these cars that are the joy of the super-man like you and me,' shouted Mr Brindley. 'Look there, "Passengers are requested not to spit on the floor." Simply an encouragement to lie on the seats and spit on the ceiling, isn't it? "Wear only Noble's wonderful boots." Suppose we did! Unless they came well up above the waist we should be prosecuted. But there's no sense of humour in this district.'

Greengrocers' shops and public-houses were now flying past the windows of the car. It began to climb a hill, and then halted.

'Here we are!' ejaculated Mr Brindley.

And he was out of the car almost before I had risen.

We strolled along a quiet street, and came to a large building with many large lighted windows, evidently some result of public effort.

'What's that place?' I demanded.

'That's the Wedgwood Institution.'

'Oh! So that's the Wedgwood Institution, is it?'

'Yes. Commonly called the Wedgwood. Museum, reading-room, public library—dirtiest books in the world, I mean physically—art school, science school. I've never explained to you why I'm chairman of the Management Committee, have I? Well, it's because the Institution is meant to foster the arts, and I happen to know nothing about 'em. I needn't tell you that architecture, literature, and music are not arts within the meaning of the act. Not much! Like to come in and see the museum for a minute? You'll have to see it in your official capacity tomorrow.'

We crossed the road, and entered an imposing portico. Just as we did so a thick stream of slouching men began to descend the steps, like a waterfall of treacle. Mr Brindley they appeared to see, but evidently I made no impression on their retinas. They bore down the steps, hands deep in pockets, sweeping over me like Fate. Even when I bounced off one of them to a lower step, he showed by no sign that the fact of my existence had reached his consciousness— simply bore irresistibly downwards. The crowd was absolutely silent. At last I gained the entrance hall.

'It's closing-time for the reading room,' said Mr Brindley.

'I'm glad I survived it,' I said.

'The truth is,' said he, 'that people who can't look after themselves don't flourish in these latitudes. But you'll be acclimatized by tomorrow. See that?'

He pointed to an alabaster tablet on which was engraved a record of the historical certainty that Mr Gladstone opened the Institution in 1868, also an extract from the speech which he delivered on that occasion.

'What do you THINK of Gladstone down here?' I demanded.

'In my official capacity I think that these deathless words are the last utterance of wisdom on the subject of the influence of the liberal arts on life. And I should advise you, in your official capacity, to think the same, unless you happen to have a fancy for having your teeth knocked down your throat.'

'I see,' I said, not sure how to take him.

'Lest you should go away with the idea that you have been visiting a rude and barbaric people, I'd better explain that that was a joke. As a matter of fact, we're rather enlightened here. The only man who stands a chance of getting his teeth knocked down his throat here is the ingenious person who started the celebrated legend of the man-and-dog fight at Hanbridge. It's a long time ago, a very long time ago; but his grey hairs won't save him from horrible tortures if we catch him. We don't mind being called immoral, we're above a bit flattered when London newspapers come out with shocking details of debauchery in the Five Towns, but we pride ourselves on our manners. I say, Aked!' His voice rose commandingly, threateningly, to an old bent, spectacled man who was ascending a broad white staircase in front of us.

'Sir!' The man turned.

'Don't turn the lights out yet in the museum.'

'No, sir! Are you coming up?' The accents were slow and tremulous.

'Yes. I have a gentleman here from the British Museum who wants to look round.'

The oldish man came deliberately down the steps, and approached us. Then his gaze, beginning at my waist, gradually rose to my hat.

'From the British Museum?' he drawled. 'I'm sure I'm very glad to meet you, sir. I'm sure it's a very great honour.'

He held out a wrinkled hand, which I shook.

'Mr Aked,' said Mr Brindley, by way of introduction. 'Been caretaker here for pretty near forty years.'

'Ever since it opened, sir,' said Aked.

We went up the white stone stairway, rather a grandiose construction for a little industrial town. It divided itself into doubling curving flights at the first landing, and its walls were covered with pictures and designs. The museum itself, a series of three communicating rooms, was about as large as a pocket-handkerchief.

'Quite small,' I said.

I gave my impression candidly, because I had already judged Mr Brindley to be the rare and precious individual who is worthy of the high honour of frankness.

'Do you think so?' he demanded quickly. I had shocked him, that was clear. His tone was unmistakable; it indicated an instinctive, involuntary protest. But he recovered himself in a flash. 'That's jealousy,' he laughed. 'All you British Museum people are the same.' Then he added, with an unsuccessful attempt to convince me that he meant what he was saying: 'Of course it is small. It's nothing, simply nothing.'

Yes, I had unwittingly found the joint in the armour of this extraordinary Midland personage. With all his irony, with all his violent humour, with all his just and unprejudiced perceptions, he had a tenderness for the Institution of which he was the dictator. He loved it. He could laugh like a god at everything in the Five Towns except this one thing. He would try to force himself to regard even this with the same lofty detachment, but he could not do it naturally.

I stopped at a case of Wedgwood ware, marked 'Perkins Collection.'

'By Jove!' I exclaimed, pointing to a vase. 'What a body!'

He was enchanted by my enthusiasm.

'Funny you should have hit on that,' said he. 'Old Daddy Perkins always called it his ewe-lamb.'

Thus spoken, the name of the greatest authority on Wedgwood ware that Europe has ever known curiously impressed me.

'I suppose you knew him?' I questioned.

'Considering that I was one of the pall-bearers at his funeral, and caught the champion cold of my life!'

'What sort of a man was he?'

'Outside Wedgwood ware he wasn't any sort of a man. He was that scourge of society, a philanthropist,' said Mr Brindley. 'He was an upright citizen, and two thousand people followed him to his grave. I'm an upright citizen, but I have no hope that two thousand people will follow me to my grave.'

'You never know what may happen,' I observed, smiling.

'No.' He shook his head. 'If you undermine the moral character of your fellow-citizens by a long course of unbridled miscellaneous philanthropy, you can have a funeral procession as long as you like, at the rate of about forty shillings a foot. But you'll never touch the great heart of the enlightened public of these boroughs in any other way. Do you imagine anyone cared a twopenny damn for Perkins's Wedgwood ware?'

'It's like that everywhere,' I said.

'I suppose it is,' he assented unwillingly.

Who can tell what was passing in the breast of Mr Brindley? I could not. At least I could not tell with any precision. I could only gather, vaguely, that what he considered the wrong- headedness, the blindness, the lack of true perception, of his public was beginning to produce in his individuality a faint trace of permanent soreness. I regretted it. And I showed my sympathy with him by asking questions about the design and construction of the museum (a late addition to the Institution), of which I happened to know that he had been the architect.

He at once became interested and interesting. Although he perhaps insisted a little too much on the difficulties which occur when original talent encounters stupidity, he did, as he walked me up and down, contrive to convey to me a notion of the creative processes of the architect in a way that was in my experience entirely novel. He was impressing me anew, and I was wondering whether he was unique of his kind or whether there existed regiments of him in this strange parcel of England.

'Now, you see this girder,' he said, looking upwards.

That's surely something of Fuge's, isn't it?' I asked, indicating a small picture in a corner, after he had finished his explanation of the functions of the girder.

As on the walls of the staircase and corridors, so on the walls here, there were many paintings, drawings, and engravings. And of course the best were here in the museum. The least uninteresting items of the collection were, speaking generally, reproductions in monotint of celebrated works, and a few second—or third-rate loan pictures from South Kensington. Aside from such matters I had noticed nothing but the usual local trivialities, gifts from one citizen or another, travel-jottings of some art-master, careful daubs of apt students without a sense of humour. The aspect of the place was exactly the customary aspect of the small provincial museum, as I have seen it in half-a-hundred towns that are not among 'the great towns'. It had the terrible trite 'museum' aspect, the aspect that brings woe and desolation to the heart of the stoutest visitor, and which seems to form part of the purgatorio of Bank-holidays, wide mouths, and stiff clothes. The movement for opening museums on Sundays is the most natural movement that could be conceived. For if ever a resort was invented and fore-ordained to chime with the true spirit of the British sabbath, that resort is the average museum. I ought to know. I do know.

But there was the incomparable Wedgwood ware, and there was the little picture by Simon Fuge. I am not going to lose my sense of perspective concerning Simon Fuge. He was not the greatest painter that ever lived, or even of his time. He had, I am ready to believe, very grave limitations. But he was a painter by himself, as all fine painters are. He had his own vision. He was Unique. He was exclusively preoccupied with the beauty and the romance of the authentic. The little picture showed all this. It was a painting, unfinished, of a girl standing at a door and evidently hesitating whether to open the door or not: a very young girl, very thin, with long legs in black stockings, and short, white, untidy frock; thin bare arms; the head thrown on one side, and the hands raised, and one foot raised, in a wonderful childish gesture—the gesture of an undecided fox-terrier. The face was an infant's face, utterly innocent; and yet Simon Fuge had somehow caught in that face a glimpse of all the future of the woman that the girl was to be, he had displayed with exquisite insolence the essential naughtiness of his vision of things. The thing was not much more than a sketch; it was a happy accident, perhaps, in some day's work of Simon Fuge's. But it was genius. When once you had yielded to it, there was no other picture in the room. It killed everything else. But, wherever it had found itself, nothing could have killed IT. Its success was undeniable, indestructible. And it glowed sombrely there on the wall, a few splashes of colour on a morsel of canvas, and it was Simon Fuge's unconscious, proud challenge to the Five Towns. It WAS Simon Fuge, at any rate all of Simon Fuge that was worth having, masterful, imperishable. And not merely was it his challenge, it was his scorn, his aristocratic disdain, his positive assurance that in the battle between them he had annihilated the Five Towns. It hung there in the very midst thereof, calmly and contemptuously waiting for the acknowledgement of his victory.

'Which?' said Mr Brindley.

That one.'

'Yes, I fancy it is,' he negligently agreed. 'Yes, it is.'

'It's not signed,' I remarked.

'It ought to be,' said Mr Brindley; then laughed, 'Too late now!'

'How did it get here?'

'Don't know. Oh! I think Mr Perkins won it in a raffle at a bazaar, and then hung it here. He did as he liked here, you know.'

I was just going to become vocal in its praise, when Mr Brindley said—

'That thing under it is a photograph of a drinking-cup for which one of our pupils won a national scholarship last year!'

Mr Aked appeared in the distance.

'I fancy the old boy wants to be off to bed,' Mr Brindley whispered kindly.

So we left the Wedgwood Institution. I began to talk to Mr Brindley about music. The barbaric attitude of the Five Towns towards great music was the theme of some very lively animadversions on his part.

VI

The Tiger was very conveniently close to the Wedgwood Institution. The Tiger had a 'yard', one of those long, shapeless expanses of the planet, partly paved with uneven cobbles and partly unsophisticated planet, without which no provincial hotel can call itself respectable. We came into it from the hinterland through a wooden doorway in a brick wall. Far off I could see one light burning. We were in the centre of Bursley, the gold angel of its Town Hall rose handsomely over the roof of the hotel in the diffused moonlight, but we might have been in the purlieus of some dubious establishment on the confines of a great seaport, where anything may happen. The yard was so deserted, so mysterious, so shut in, so silent, that, really, infamous characters ought to have rushed out at us from the obscurity of shadows, and felled us to the earth with no other attendant phenomenon than a low groan. There are places where one seems to feel how thin and brittle is the crust of law and order. Why one should be conscious of this in the precincts of such a house as the Tiger, which I was given to understand is as respectable as the parish church, I do not know. But I have experienced a similar feeling in the yards of other provincial hotels that were also as correct as parish churches. We passed a dim fly, with its shafts slanting forlornly to the ground, and a wheelbarrow. Both looked as though they had been abandoned for ever. Then we came to the lamp, which illuminated a door, and on the door was a notice: 'Private Bar. Billiards.'

I am not a frequenter of convivial haunts. I should not dare to penetrate alone into a private bar; when I do enter a private bar it is invariably under the august protection of an habitue, and it is invariably with the idea that at last I am going to see life. Often has this illusion been shattered, but each time it perfectly renewed itself. So I followed the bold Mr Brindley into the private bar of the Tiger.

It was a small and low room. I instinctively stooped, though there was no necessity for me to stoop. The bar had no peculiarity. It can be described in a breath: Three perpendicular planes. Back plane, bottles arranged exactly like books on bookshelves; middle plane, the upper halves of two women dressed in tight black; front plane, a counter, dotted with glasses, and having strange areas of zinc. Reckon all that as the stage, and the rest of the room as auditorium. But the stage of a private bar is more mysterious than the stage of a theatre. You are closer to it, and yet it is far less approachable. The edge of the counter is more sacred than the footlights. Impossible to imagine yourself leaping over it. Impossible to imagine yourself in that cloistered place behind it. Impossible to imagine how the priestesses got themselves into that place, or that they ever leave it. They are always there; they are always the same. You may go into a theatre when it is empty and dark; but did you ever go into a private bar that was empty and dark? A private bar is as eternal as the hills, as changeless as the monomania of a madman, as mysterious as sorcery. Always the same order of bottles, the same tinkling, the same popping, the same time-tables, and the same realistic pictures of frothing champagne on the walls, the same advertisements on the same ash- trays on the counter, the same odour that wipes your face like a towel the instant you enter; and the same smiles, the same gestures, the same black fabric stretched to tension over the same impressive mammiferous phenomena of the same inexplicable creatures who apparently never eat and never sleep, imprisoned for life in the hallowed and mystic hollow between the bottles and the zinc.

In a tone almost inaudible in its discretion, Mr Brindley let fall to me as he went in—

This is she.'

She was not quite the ordinary barmaid. Nor, as I learnt afterwards, was she considered to be the ordinary barmaid. She was something midway in importance between the wife of the new proprietor and the younger woman who stood beside her in the cloister talking to a being that resembled a commercial traveller. It was the younger woman who was the ordinary barmaid; she had bright hair, and the bright vacant stupidity which, in my narrow experience, barmaids so often catch like an infectious disease from their clients. But Annie Brett was different. I can best explain how she impressed me by saying that she had the mien of a handsome married woman of forty with a coquettish and superficially emotional past, but also with a daughter who is just going into long skirts. I have known one or two such women. They have been beautiful; they are still handsome at a distance of twelve feet. They are rather effusive; they think they know life, when as a fact their instinctive repugnance for any form of truth has prevented them from acquiring even the rudiments of the knowledge of life. They are secretly preoccupied by the burning question of obesity. They flatter, and they will pay any price for flattery. They are never sincere, not even with themselves; they never, during the whole of their existence, utter a sincere word, even in anger they coldly exaggerate. They are always frothing at the mouth with ecstasy. They adore everything, including God; go to church carrying a prayer-book and hymn-book in separate volumes, and absolutely fawn on the daughter. They are stylish— and impenetrable. But there is something about them very wistful and tragic.

In another social stratum, Miss Annie Brett might have been such a woman. Without doubt nature had intended her for the role. She was just a little ample, with broad shoulders and a large head and a lot of dark chestnut hair; a large mouth, and large teeth. She had earrings, a brooch, and several rings; also a neat originality of cuffs that would not have been permitted to an ordinary barmaid. As for her face, there were crow's-feet, and a mole (which had selected with infinite skill a site on her chin), and a general degeneracy of complexion; but it was an effective face. The little thing of twenty-three or so by her side had all the cruel advantages of youth and was not ugly; but she was 'killed' by Annie Brett. Miss Brett had a maternal bust. Indeed, something of the maternal resided in all of her that was visible above the zinc. She must have been about forty; that is to say, apparently older than the late Simon Fuge. Nevertheless, I could conceive her, even now, speciously picturesque in a boat at midnight on a moonstruck water. Had she been on the stage she would have been looking forward to ingenue parts for another five years yet—such was her durable sort of effectiveness. Yes, she indubitably belonged to the ornamental half of the universe.

'So this is one of them!' I said to myself.

I tried to be philosophical; but at heart I was profoundly disappointed. I did not know what I had expected; but I had not expected THAT. I was well aware that a thing written always takes on a quality which does not justly appertain to it. I had not expected, therefore, to see an odalisque, a houri, an ideal toy or the remains of an ideal toy; I had not expected any kind of obvious brilliancy, nor a subtle charm that would haunt my memory for evermore. On the other hand, I had not expected the banal, the perfectly commonplace. And I think that Miss Annie Brett was the most banal person that it has pleased Fate to send into my life. I knew that instantly. She was a condemnation of Simon Fuge. SHE, one of the 'wonderful creatures who had played so large a part' in the career of Simon Fuge! Sapristi! Still, she WAS one of the wonderful creatures, etc. She HAD floated o'er the bosom of the lake with a great artist. She HAD received his homage. She HAD stirred his feelings. She HAD shared with him the magic of the night. I might decry her as I would; she had known how to cast a spell over him—she and the other one! Something there in her which had captured him and, seemingly, held him captive.

'Good-EVENING, Mr Brindley,' she expanded. 'You're quite a stranger.' And she embraced me also in the largeness of her welcome.

'It just happens,' said Mr Brindley, 'that I was here last night. But you weren't.'

'Were you now!' she exclaimed, as though learning a novel fact of the most passionate interest. 'The truth is, I had to leave the bar to Miss Slaney last night. Mrs Moorcroft was ill—and the baby only six weeks old, you know—and I wouldn't leave her. No, I wouldn't.'

It was plain that in Miss Annie Brett's opinion there was only one really capable intelligence in the Tiger. This glimpse of her capability, this out-leaping of the latent maternal in her, completely destroyed for the moment my vision of her afloat on the bosom of the lake.

'I see,' said Mr Brindley kindly. Then he turned to me with characteristic abruptness. 'Well, give it a name, Mr Loring.'

Such is my simplicity that I did not immediately comprehend his meaning. For a fraction of a second I thought of the baby. Then I perceived that he was merely employing one of the sacred phrases, sanctified by centuries of usage, of the private bar. I had already drunk mercurey, green Chartreuse, and coffee. I had a violent desire not to drink anything more. I knew my deplorable tomorrows. Still, I would have drunk hot milk, cold water, soda water, or tea. Why should I not have had what I did not object to having? Herein lies another mystery of the private bar. One could surely order tea or milk or soda water from a woman who left everything to tend a mother with a six-weeks-old baby! But no. One could not. As Miss Annie Brett smiled at me pointedly, and rubbed her ringed hands, and kept on smiling with her terrific mechanical effusiveness, I lost all my self control; I would have resigned myself to a hundred horrible tomorrows under the omnipotent, inexplicable influence of the private bar. I ejaculated, as though to the manner born—

'Irish.'

It proved to have been rather clever of me, showing as it did a due regard for convention combined with a pretty idiosyncrasy. Mr Brindley was clearly taken aback. The idea struck him as a new one. He reflected, and then enthusiastically exclaimed—

'Dashed if I don't have Irish too!'

And Miss Brett, delighted by this unexpected note of Irish in the long, long symphony of Scotch, charged our glasses with gusto. I sipped, death in my heart, and rakishness in my face and gesture. Mr Brindley raised his glass respectfully to Miss Annie Brett, and I did the same. Those two were evidently good friends.

She led the conversation with hard, accustomed ease. When I say 'hard' I do not in the least mean unsympathetic. But her sympathetic quality was toughened by excessive usage, like the hand of a charwoman. She spoke of the vagaries of the Town Hall clock, the health of Mr Brindley's children, the price of coal, the incidence of the annual wakes, the bankruptcy of the draper next door, and her own sciatica, all in the same tone of metallic tender solicitude. Mr Brindley adopted an entirely serious attitude towards her. If I had met him there and nowhere else I should have taken him for a dignified mediocrity, little better than a fool, but with just enough discretion not to give himself away. I said nothing. I was shy. I always am shy in a bar. Out of her cold, cold roving eye Miss Brett watched me, trying to add me up and not succeeding. She must have perceived, however, that I was not like a fish in water.

There was a pause in the talk, due, I think, to Miss Annie Brett's preoccupation with what was going on between Miss Slaney, the ordinary barmaid, and her commercial traveller. The commercial traveller, if he was one, was reading something from a newspaper to Miss Slaney in an indistinct murmur, and with laughter in his voice.

'By the way,' said Mr Brindley, 'you used to know Simon Fuge, didn't you?'

'Old Simon Fuge!' said Miss Brett. 'Yes; after the brewery company took the Blue Bell at Cauldon over from him, I used to be there. He would come in sometimes. Such a nice queer old man!'

'I mean the son,' said Mr Brindley.

'Oh yes,' she answered. 'I knew young Mr Simon too.' A slight hesitation, and then: 'Of course!' Another hesitation. 'Why?'

'Nothing,' said Mr Brindley. 'Only he's dead.'

'You don't mean to say he's dead?' she exclaimed.

'Day before yesterday, in Italy,' said Mr Brindley ruthlessly.

Miss Annie Brett's manner certainly changed. It seemed almost to become natural and unecstatic.

'I suppose it will be in the papers?' she ventured.

'It's in the London paper.'

'Well I never!' she muttered.

'A long time, I should think, since he was in this part of the world,' said Mr Brindley. 'When did YOU last see him?'

He was exceedingly skilful, I considered.

She put the back of her hand over her mouth, and bending her head slightly and lowering her eyelids, gazed reflectively at the counter.

'It was once when a lot of us went to Ilam,' she answered quietly. 'The St Luke's lot, YOU know.'

'Oh!' cried Mr Brindley, apparently startled. 'The St Luke's lot?'

'Yes.'

'How came he to go with you?'

'He didn't go with us. He was there—stopping there, I suppose.'

'Why, I believe I remember hearing something about that,' said Mr Brindley cunningly. 'Didn't he take you out in a boat?'

A very faint dark crimson spread over the face of Miss Annie Brett. It could not be called a blush, but it was as like a blush as was possible to her. The phenomenon, as I could see from his eyes, gave Mr Brindley another shock.

'Yes,' she replied. 'Sally was there as well.'

Then a silence, during which the commercial traveller could be heard reading from the newspaper.

'When was that?' gently asked Mr Brindley.

'Don't ask ME when it was, Mr Brindley,' she answered nervously. 'It's ever so long ago. What did he die of?'

'Don't know.'

Miss Annie Brett opened her mouth to speak, and did not speak. There were tears in her reddened eyes. I felt very awkward, and I think that Mr Brindley also felt awkward. But I was glad. Those moist eyes caused me a thrill. There was after all some humanity in Miss Annie Brett. Yes, she had after all floated on the bosom of the lake with Simon Fuge. The least romantic of persons, she had yet felt romance. If she had touched Simon Fuge, Simon Fuge had touched her. She had memories. Once she had lived. I pictured her younger. I sought in her face the soft remains of youthfulness. I invented languishing poses for her in the boat. My imagination was equal to the task of seeing her as Simon Fuge saw her. I did so see her. I recalled Simon Fuge's excited description of the long night in the boat, and I could reconstitute the night from end to end. And there the identical creature stood before me, the creature who had set fire to Simon Fuge, one of the 'wonderful creatures' of the Gazette, ageing, hardened, banal, but momentarily restored to the empire of romance by those unshed, glittering tears. As an experience it was worth having.

She could not speak, and we did not. I heard the commercial traveller reading: '"The motion was therefore carried by twenty- five votes to nineteen, and the Countess of Chell promised that the whole question of the employment of barmaids should be raised at the next meeting of the B.W.T.S." There! what do you think of that?'

Miss Annie Brett moved quickly towards the commercial traveller.

'I'll tell you what *I* think of it,' she said, with ecstatic resentment. 'I think it's just shameful! Why should the Countess of Chell want to rob a lot of respectable young ladies of their living? I can tell you they're just as respectable as the Countess of Chell is—yes, and perhaps more, by all accounts. I think people do well to call her "Interfering Iris". When she's robbed them of their living, what does she expect them to do? Is she going to keep them? Then what does she expect them to do?'

The commercial traveller was inept enough to offer a jocular reply, and then he found himself involved in the morass of 'the whole question'. He, and we also, were obliged to hear in immense detail Miss Annie Brett's complete notions of the movement for the abolition of barmaids. The subject was heavy on her mind, and she lifted it off. Simon Fuge was relinquished; he dropped like a stone into the pool of forgetfulness. And yet, strange as it seems, she was assuredly not sincere in the expression of her views on the question of barmaids. She held no real views. She merely persuaded herself that she held them. When the commercial traveller, who was devoid of sense, pointed out that it was not proposed to rob anybody of a livelihood, and that existent barmaids would be permitted to continue to grace the counters of their adoption, she grew frostily vicious. The commercial traveller decided to retire and play billiards. Mr Brindley and I in our turn departed. I was extremely disappointed by this sequel.

'Ah!' breathed Mr Brindley when we were outside, in front of the Town Hall. 'She was quite right about that clock.'

After that we turned silently into a long illuminated street which rose gently. The boxes of light were flashing up and down it, but otherwise it seemed to be quite deserted. Mr Brindley filled a pipe and lit it as he walked. The way in which that man kept the match alight in a fresh breeze made me envious. I could conceive myself rivalling his exploits in cigarette-making, the purchase of rare books, the interpretation of music, even (for a wager) the drinking of beer, but I knew that I should never be able to keep a match alight in a breeze. He threw the match into the mud, and in the mud it continued miraculously to burn with a large flame, as though still under his magic dominion. There are some things that baffle the reasoning faculty. 'Well,' I said, 'she must have been a pretty woman once.'

'"Pretty," by God!' he replied, 'she was beautiful. She was considered the finest piece in Hanbridge at one time. And let me tell you we're supposed to have more than our share of good looks in the Five Towns.'

'What—the women, you mean?'

'Yes.'

'And she never married?'

'No.'

'Nor—anything?'

'Oh no,' he said carelessly.

'But you don't mean to tell me she's never—' I was just going to exclaim, but I did not, I said: 'And it's her sister who is Mrs Colclough?'

'Yes.' He seemed to be either meditative or disinclined to talk. However, my friends have sometimes hinted to me that when my curiosity is really aroused, I am capable of indiscretions.

'So one sister rattles about in an expensive motor-car, and the other serves behind a bar!' I observed.

He glanced at me.

'I expect it's a bit difficult for you to understand,' he answered; 'but you must remember you're in a democratic district. You told me once you knew Exeter. Well, this isn't a cathedral town. It's about a century in front of any cathedral town in the world. Why, my good sir, there's practically no such thing as class distinction here. Both my grandfathers were working potters. Colclough's father was a joiner who finished up as a builder. If Colclough makes money and chooses to go to Paris and get the best motor-car he can, why in Hades shouldn't his wife ride in it? If he is fond of music and can play like the devil, that isn't his sister-in-law's fault, is it? His wife was a dressmaker, at least she was a dressmaker's assistant. If she suits him, what's the matter?'

'But I never suggested—'

'Excuse me,' he stopped me, speaking with careful and slightly exaggerated calmness, 'I think you did. If the difference in the situations of the two sisters didn't strike you as very extraordinary, what did you mean?'

'And isn't it extraordinary?' I demanded.

'It wouldn't be considered so in any reasonable society,' he insisted. 'The fact is, my good sir, you haven't yet quite got rid of Exeter. I do believe this place will do you good. Why, damn it! Colclough didn't marry both sisters. You think he might keep the other sister? Well, he might. But suppose his wife had half-a-dozen sisters, should he keep them all! I can tell you we're just like the rest of the world, we find no difficulty whatever in spending all the money we make. I dare say Colclough would be ready enough to keep his sister-in-law. I've never asked him. But I'm perfectly certain that his sister-in-law wouldn't be kept. Not much! You don't know these women down here, my good sir. She's earned her living at one thing or another all her life, and I reckon she'll keep on earning it till she drops. She is, without exception, the most exasperating female I ever came across, and that's saying something; but I will give her THAT credit: she's mighty independent.'

'How exasperating?' I asked, surprised to hear this from him.

'*I* don't know. But she is. If she was my wife I should kill her one night. Don't you know what I mean?'

'Yes, I quite agree with you,' I said. 'But you seemed to be awfully good friends with her.'

'No use being anything else. No woman that it ever pleased Providence to construct is going to frighten me away from the draught Burton that you can get at the Tiger. Besides, she can't help it. She was born like that.'

'She TALKS quite ordinarily,' I remarked.

'Oh! It isn't what she says, particularly. It's HER. Either you like her or you don't like her. Now Colclough thinks she's all right. In fact, he admires her.'

'There's one thing,' I said, 'she jolly nearly cried tonight.'

'Purely mechanical!' said Mr Brindley with cruel curtness.

What seemed to me singular was that the relations which had existed between Miss Annie Brett and Simon Fuge appeared to have no interest whatever for Mr Brindley. He had not even referred to them.

'You were just beginning to draw her out,' I ventured.

'No,' he replied; 'I thought I'd just see what she'd say. No one ever did draw that woman out.'

I had completely lost my vision of her in the boat, but somehow that declaration of his, 'no one ever did draw that woman out', partially restored the vision to me. It seemed to invest her with agreeable mystery.

'And the other sister—Mrs Colclough?' I questioned.

'I'm taking you to see her as fast as I can,' he answered. His tone implied further: 'I've just humoured one of your whims, now for the other.'

'But tell me something about her.'

'She's the best bridge-player—woman, that is—in Bursley. But she will only play every other night for fear the habit should get hold of her. There you've got her.'

'Younger than Miss Brett?'

'Younger,' said Mr Brindley. 'She isn't the same sort of person, is she?'

'She is not,' said Mr Brindley. And his tone implied: 'Thank God for it!'

Very soon afterwards, at the top of a hill, he drew me into the garden of a large house which stood back from the road.

VII

It was quite a different sort of house from Mr Brindley's. One felt that immediately on entering the hall, which was extensive. There was far more money and considerably less taste at large in that house than in the other. I noticed carved furniture that must have been bought with a coarse and a generous hand; and on the walls a diptych by Marcus Stone portraying the course of true love clingingly draped. It was just like Exeter or Onslow Square. But the middle-aged servant who received us struck at once the same note as had sounded so agreeably at Mr Brindley's. She seemed positively glad to see us; our arrival seemed to afford her a peculiar and violent pleasure, as though the hospitality which we were about to accept was in some degree hers too. She robbed us of our hats with ecstasy.

Then Mr Colclough appeared.

'Delighted you've come, Mr Loring!' he said, shaking my hand again. He said it with fervour. He obviously was delighted. The exercise of hospitality was clearly the chief joy of his life; at least, if he had a greater it must have been something where keenness was excessive beyond the point of pleasure, as some joys are. 'How do, Bob? Your missis has just come.' He was still in his motoring clothes.

Mr Brindley, observing my gaze transiently on the Marcus Stones, said: 'I know what you're looking for; you're looking for "Saul's Soul's Awakening". We don't keep it in the window; you'll see it inside.'

'Bob's always rotting me about my pictures,' Mr Colclough smiled indulgently. He seemed big enough to eat his friend, and his rich, heavy voice rolled like thunder about the hall. 'Come along in, will you?'

'Half-a-second, Ol,' Mr Brindley called in a conspiratorial tone, and, turning to me: Tell him THE Limerick. You know.'

'The one about the hayrick?'

Mr Brindley nodded.

There were three heads close together for a space of twenty seconds or so, and then a fearful explosion happened—the unique, tremendous laughter of Mr Colclough, which went off like a charge of melinite and staggered the furniture.

'Now, now!' a feminine voice protested from an unseen interior.

I was taken to the drawing-room, an immense apartment with an immense piano black as midnight in it. At the further end two women were seated close together in conversation, and I distinctly heard the name 'Fuge'. One of them was Mrs Brindley, in a hat. The other, a very big and stout woman, in an elaborate crimson garment that resembled a teagown, rose and came to meet me with extended hand.

'My wife—Mr Loring,' said Mr Oliver Colclough.

'So glad to meet you,' she said, beaming on me with all her husband's pleasure. 'Come and sit between Mrs Brindley and me, near the window, and keep us in order. Don't you find it very close? There are at least a hundred cats in the garden.'

One instantly perceived that ceremonial stiffness could not exist in the same atmosphere with Mrs Oliver Colclough. During the whole time I spent in her house there was never the slightest pause in the conversation. Mrs Oliver Colclough prevented nobody from talking, but she would gladly use up every odd remnant of time that was not employed by others. No scrap was too small for her.

'So this is the other one!' I said to myself. 'Well, give me this one!'

Certainly there was a resemblance between the two, in the general formation of the face, and the shape of the shoulders; but it is astonishing that two sisters can differ as these did, with a profound and vital difference. In Mrs Colclough there was no coquetterie, no trace of that more-than-half-suspicious challenge to a man that one feels always in the type to which her sister belonged. The notorious battle of the sexes was assuredly carried on by her in a spirit of frank muscular gaiety—she could, I am sure, do her share of fighting. Put her in a boat on the bosom of the lake under starlight, and she would not by a gesture, a tone, a glance, convey mysterious nothings to you, a male. She would not be subtly changed by the sensuous influences of the situation; she would always be the same plump and earthly piece of candour. Even if she were in love with you, she would not convey mysterious nothings in such circumstances. If she were in love with you she would most clearly convey unmysterious and solid somethings. I was convinced that the contributing cause to the presence of the late Simon Fuge in the boat on Ilam Lake on the historic night was Annie the superior barmaid, and not Sally of the automobile. But Mrs Colclough, if not beautiful, was a very agreeable creation. Her amplitude gave at first sight an exaggerated impression of her age; but this departed after more careful inspection. She could not have been more than thirty. She was very dark, with plenteous and untidy black hair, thick eyebrows, and a slight moustache. Her eyes were very vivacious, and her gestures, despite that bulk, quick and graceful. She was happy; her ideals were satisfied; it was probably happiness that had made her stout. Her massiveness was apparently no grief to her; she had fallen into the carelessness which is too often the pitfall of women who, being stout, are content.

'How do, missis?' Mr Brindley greeted her, and to his wife, 'How do, missis? But, look here, bright star, this gadding about is all very well, but what about those precious kids of yours? None of 'em dead yet, I hope.'

'Don't be silly, Bob.'

'I've been over to your house,' Mrs Colclough put in. 'Of course it isn't mumps. The child's as right as rain. So I brought Mary back with me.'

'Well,' said Mr Brindley, 'for a woman who's never had any children your knowledge of children beggars description. What you aren't sure you know about them isn't knowledge. However—'

'Listen,' Mrs Colclough replied, with a delightful throwingdown of the glove. 'I'll bet you a level sovereign that child hasn't got the mumps. So there! And Oliver will guarantee to pay you.'

'Aye!' said Mr Colclough; 'I'll back my wife any day.'

'Don't bet, Bob,' Mrs Brindley enjoined her husband excitedly in her high treble.

'I won't,' said Mr Brindley.

'Now let's sit down.' Mrs Colclough addressed me with particular, confidential grace.

We three exactly filled the sofa. I have often sat between two women, but never with such calm, unreserved, unapprehensive comfortableness as I experienced between Mrs Colclough and Mrs Brindley. It was just as if I had known them for years.

'You'll make a mess of that, Ol,' said Mr Brindley.

The other two men were at some distance, in front of a table, on which were two champagne bottles and five glasses, and a plate of cakes. 'Well,' I said to myself, 'I'm not going to have any champagne, anyhow. Mercurey! Green Chartreuse! Irish whisky! And then champagne! And a morning's hard work tomorrow! No!'

Plop! A cork flew up and bounced against the ceiling.

Mr Colclough carefully emptied the bottle into the glasses, of which Mr Brindley seized two and advanced with one in either hand for the women. It was the host who offered a glass to me.

'No, thanks very much, I really can't,' I said in a very firm tone.

My tone was so firm that it startled them. They glanced at each other with alarmed eyes, like simple people confronted by an inexplicable phenomenon. 'But look here, mister!' said Mr Colclough, pained, 'we've got this out specially for you. You don't suppose this is our usual tipple, do you?'

I yielded. I could do no less than sacrifice myself to their enchanting instinctive kindness of heart. 'I shall be dead tomorrow,' I said to myself; 'but I shall have lived tonight.' They were relieved, but I saw that I had given them a shock from which they could not instantaneously recover. Therefore I began with a long pull, to reassure them.

'Mrs Brindley has been telling me that Simon Fuge is dead,' said Mrs Colclough brightly, as though Mrs Brindley had been telling her that the price of mutton had gone down.

I perceived that those two had been talking over Simon Fuge, after their fashion.

'Oh yes,' I responded.

'Have you got that newspaper in your pocket, Mr Loring?' asked Mrs Brindley.

I had.

'No,' I said, feeling in my pockets; 'I must have left it at your house.'

'Well,' she said, 'that's strange. I looked for it to show it to Mrs Colclough, but I couldn't see it.'

This was not surprising. I did not want Mrs Colclough to read the journalistic obituary until she had given me her own obituary of Fuge.

'It must be somewhere about,' I said; and to Mrs Colclough: 'I suppose you knew him pretty well?'

'Oh, bless you, no! I only met him once.'

'At Ilam?'

'Yes. What are you going to do, Oliver?'

Her husband was opening the piano.

'Bob and I are just going to have another smack at that Brahms.'

'You don't expect us to listen, do you?'

'I expect you to do what pleases you, missis,' said he. 'I should be a bigger fool than I am if I expected anything else.' Then he smiled at me. 'No! Just go on talking. Ol and I'll drown you easy enough. Quite short! Back in five minutes.'

The two men placed each his wine-glass on the space on the piano designed for a candlestick, lighted cigars, and sat down to play.

'Yes,' Mrs Colclough resumed, in a lower, more confidential tone, to the accompaniment of the music. 'You see, there was a whole party of us there, and Mr Fuge was staying at the hotel, and of course he knew several of us.'

'And he took you out in a boat?'

'Me and Annie? Yes. Just as it was getting dusk he came up to us and asked us if we'd go for a row. Eh, I can hear him asking us now! I asked him if he could row, and he was quite angry. So we went, to quieten him.' She paused, and then laughed.

'Sally!' Mrs Brindley protested. 'You know he's dead!'

'Yes.' She admitted the rightness of the protest. 'But I can't help it. I was just thinking how he got his feet wet in pushing the boat off.' She laughed again. 'When we were safely off, someone came down to the shore and shouted to Mr Fuge to bring the boat back. You know his quick way of talking.' (Here she began to imitate Fuge.) '"I've quarrelled with the man this boat belongs to. Awful feud! Fact is, I'm in a hostile country here!" And a lot more like that. It seemed he had quarrelled with everybody in Ilam. He wasn't sure if the landlord of the hotel would let him sleep there again. He told us all about all his quarrels, until he dropped one of the oars. I shall never forget how funny he looked in the moonlight when he dropped the oar. "There, that's your fault!" he said. "You make me talk too much about myself, and I get excited." He kept striking matches to look for the oar, and turning the boat round and round with the other oar. "Last match!" he said. "We shall never see land tonight." Then he found the oar again. He considered we were saved. Then he began to tell us about his aunt. "You know I'd no business to be here. I came down from London for my aunt's funeral, and here I am in a boat at night with two pretty girls!" He said the funeral had taught him one thing, and that was that black neckties were the only possible sort of necktie. He said the greatest worry of his life had always been neckties; but he wouldn't have to worry any more, and so his aunt hadn't died for nothing. I assure you he kept on talking about neckties. I assure you, Mr Loring, I went to sleep—at least I dozed—and when I woke up he was still talking about neckties. But then his feet began to get cold. I suppose it was because they were wet. The way he grumbled about his feet being cold! I remember he turned his coat collar up. He wanted to get on shore and walk, but he'd taken us a long way up the lake by that time, and he saw we were absolutely lost. So he put the oars in the boat and stood up and stamped his feet. It might have upset the boat.'

'How did it end?' I inquired.

'Well, Annie and I caught the train, but only just. You see it was a special train, so they kept it for us, otherwise we should have been in a nice fix.'

'So you have special trains in these parts?'

'Why, of course! It was the annual outing of the teachers of St Luke's Sunday School and their friends, you see. So we had a special train.'

At this point the duettists came to the end of a movement, and Mr Brindley leaned over to us from his stool, glass in hand.

'The railway company practically owns Ilam,' he explained, 'and so they run it for all they're worth. They made the lake, to feed the canals, when they bought the canals from the canal company. It's an artificial lake, and the railway runs alongside it. A very good scheme of the company's. They started out to make Ilam a popular resort, and they've made it a popular resort, what with special trains and things. But try to get a special train to any other place on their rotten system, and you'll soon see!'

'How big is the lake?' I asked.

'How long is it, Ol?' he demanded of Colclough. 'A couple of miles?'

'Not it! About a mile. Adagio!'

They proceeded with Brahms.

'He ran with you all the way to the station, didn't he?' Mrs Brindley suggested to Mrs Colclough.

'I should just say he did!' Mrs Colclough concurred. 'He wanted to get warm, and then he was awfully afraid lest we should miss it.'

'I thought you were on the lake practically all night!' I exclaimed.

'All night! Well, I don't know what you call all night. But I was back in Bursley before eleven o'clock, I'm sure.'

I then contrived to discover the Gazette in an unsearched pocket, and I gave it to Mrs Colclough to read. Mrs Brindley looked over her shoulder.

There was no slightest movement of depreciation on Mrs Colclough's part. She amiably smiled as she perused the GAZETTE'S version of Fuge's version of the lake episode. Here was the attitude of the woman whose soul is like crystal. It seems to me that most women would have blushed, or dissented, or simulated anger, or failed to conceal vanity. But Mrs Coclough might have been reading a fairy tale, for any emotion she displayed.

'Yes,' she said blandly; 'from the things Annie used to tell me about him sometimes, I should say that was just how he WOULD talk. They seem to have thought quite a lot of him in London, then?'

'Oh, rather!' I said. 'I suppose your sister knew him pretty well?'

'Annie? I don't know. She knew him.'

I distinctly observed a certain self-consciousness in Mrs Colclough as she made this reply. Mrs Brindley had risen and with wifely attentiveness was turning over the music page for her husband.

VIII

Soon afterwards, for me, the night began to grow fantastic; it took on the colour of a gigantic adventure. I do not suppose that either Mr Brindley or Mr Colclough, or the other person who presently arrived, regarded it as anything but a pleasant conviviality, but to a man of my constitution and habits it was an almost incredible occurrence. The other person was the book- collecting doctor. He arrived with a discreet tap on the window at midnight, to spend the evening. Mrs Brindley had gone home and Mrs Colclough had gone to bed. The book-collecting doctor refused champagne; he was, in fact, very rude to champagne in general. He had whisky. And those astonishing individuals, Messieurs Brindley and Colclough, secretly convinced of the justice of the attack on champagne, had whisky too. And that still most astonishing individual, Loring of the B.M., joined them. It was the hour of limericks. Limericks were demanded for the diversion of the doctor, and I furnished them. We then listened to the tale of the doctor's experiences that day amid the sturdy, natural-minded population of a muling village not far from Bursley. Seldom have I had such a bath in the pure fluid of human nature. All sense of time was lost. I lived in an eternity. I could not suggest to my host that we should depart. I could, however, decline more whisky. And I could, given the chance, discourse with gay despair concerning the miserable wreck that I should be on the morrow in consequence of this high living. I asked them how I could be expected, in such a state, to judge delicate points of expertise in earthenware. I gave them a brief sketch of my customary evening, and left them to compare it with that evening. The doctor perceived that I was serious. He gazed at me with pity, as if to say: 'Poor frail southern organism! It ought to be in bed, with nothing inside it but tea!' What he did actually say was: 'You come round to my place, I'll soon put you right!' 'Can you stop me from having a headache tomorrow?' I eagerly asked. 'I think so,' he said with calm northern confidence.

At some later hour Mr Brindley and I 'went round'. Mr Colclough would not come. He bade me good-bye, as his wife had done, with the most extraordinary kindness, the most genuine sorrow at quitting me, the most genuine pleasure in the hope of seeing me again.

'There are three thousand books in this room!' I said to myself, as I stood in the doctor's electrically lit library.

'What price this for a dog?' Mr Brindley drew my attention to an aristocratic fox-terrier that lay on the hearth. 'Well, Titus! Is it sleepy? Well, well! How many firsts has he won, doctor?'

'Six,' said the doctor. 'I'll just fix you up, to begin with,' he turned to me.

After I had been duly fixed up ('This'll help you to sleep, and THIS'll placate your "god",' said the doctor), I saw to my intense surprise that another 'evening' was to be instantly superimposed on the 'evening' at Mr Colclough's. The doctor and Mr Brindley carefully and deliberately lighted long cigars, and sank deeply into immense arm-chairs; and so I imitated them as well as I could in my feeble southern way. We talked books. We just simply enumerated books without end, praising or damning them, and arranged authors in neat pews, like cattle in classes at an agricultural show. No pastime is more agreeable to people who have the book disease, and none more quickly fleets the hours, and none is more delightfully futile.

Ages elapsed, and suddenly, like a gun discharging, Mr Brindley said—

'We must go!'

Of all things that happened this was the most astonishing.

We did go.

'By the way, doc.,' said Mr Brindley, in the doctor's wide porch, 'I forgot to tell you that Simon Fuge is dead.'

'Is he?' said the doctor.

'Yes. You've got a couple of his etchings, haven't you?'

'No,' said the doctor. 'I had. But I sold them several months ago.'

'Oh!' said Mr Brindley negligently; 'I didn't know. Well, so long!'

We had a few hundred yards to walk down the silent, wide street, where the gas-lamps were burning with the strange, endless patience that gas-lamps have. The stillness of a provincial town at night is quite different from that of London; we might have been the only persons alive in England.

Except for a feeling of unreality, a feeling that the natural order of things had been disturbed by some necromancer, I was perfectly well the same morning at breakfast, as the doctor had predicted I should be. When I expressed to Mr Brindley my stupefaction at this happy sequel, he showed a polite but careless inability to follow my line of thought. It appeared that he was always well at breakfast, even when he did stay up 'a little later than usual'. It appeared further that he always breakfasted at a quarter to nine, and read the Manchester Guardian during the meal, to which his wife did or did not descend—according to the moods of the nursery; and that he reached his office at a quarter to ten. That morning the mood of the nursery was apparently unpropitious. He and I were alone. I begged him not to pretermit his GUARDIAN, but to examine it and give me the news. He agreed, scarcely unwilling.

'There's a paragraph in the London correspondence about Fuge,' he announced from behind the paper.

'What do they say about him?'

'Nothing particular.'

'Now I want to ask you something,' I said.

I had been thinking a good deal about the sisters and Simon Fuge. And in spite of everything that I had heard—in spite even of the facts that the lake had been dug by a railway company, and that the excursion to the lake had been an excursion of Sunday-school teachers and their friends—I was still haunted by certain notions concerning Simon Fuge and Annie Brett. Annie Brett's flush, her unshed tears; and the self-consciousness shown by Mrs Colclough when I had pointedly mentioned her sister's name in connection with Simon Fuge's: these were surely indications! And then the doctor's recitals of manners in the immediate neighbourhood of Bursley went to support my theory that even in Staffordshire life was very much life.

'What?' demanded Mr Brindley.

'Was Miss Brett ever Simon Fuge's mistress?'

At that moment Mrs Brindley, miraculously fresh and smiling, entered the room.

'Wife,' said Mr Brindley, without giving her time to greet me, 'what do you think he's just asked me?'

'*I* don't know.'

'He's just asked me if Annie Brett was ever Simon Fuge's mistress.'

She sank into a chair.

'Annie BRETT?' She began to laugh gently. 'Oh! Mr Loring, you really are too funny!' She yielded to her emotions. It may be said that she laughed as they can laugh in the Five Towns. She cried. She had to wipe away the tears of laughter.

'What on earth made you think so?' she inquired, after recovery.

'I—had an idea,' I said lamely. 'He always made out that one of those two sisters was so much to him, and I knew it couldn't be Mrs Colclough.'

'Well,' she said, 'ask anybody down here, ANY-body! And see what they'll say.'

'No,' Mr Brindley put in, 'don't go about asking ANY-body. You might get yourself disliked. But you may take it it isn't true.'

'Most certainly,' his wife concurred with seriousness.

'We reckon to know something about Simon Fuge down here,' Mr Brindley added. 'Also about the famous Annie.'

'He must have flirted with her a good bit, anyhow,' I said.

'Oh, FLIRT!' ejaculated Mr Brindley.

I had a sudden dazzling vision of the great truth that the people of the Five Towns have no particular use for half-measures in any department of life. So I accepted the final judgement with meekness.

IX

I returned to London that evening, my work done, and the muncipality happily flattered by my judgement of the slip- decorated dishes. Mr Brindley had found time to meet me at the midday meal, and he had left his office earlier than usual in order to help me to drink his wife's afternoon tea. About an hour later he picked up my little bag, and said that he should accompany me to the little station in the midst of the desert of cinders and broken crockery, and even see me as far as Knype, where I had to take the London express. No, there are no half-measures in the Five Towns. Mrs Brindley stood on her doorstep, with her eldest infant on her shoulders, and waved us off. The infant cried, expressing his own and his mother's grief at losing a guest. It seems as if people are born hospitable in the Five Towns.

We had not walked more than a hundred yards up the road when a motor-car thundered down upon us from the opposite direction. It was Mr Colclough's, and Mr Colclough was driving it. Mr Brindley stopped his friend with the authoritative gesture of a policeman.

'Where are you going, Ol?'

'Home, lad. Sorry you're leaving us so soon, Mr Loring.'

'You're mistaken, my boy,' said Mr Brindley. 'You're just going to run us down to Knype station, first.'

'I must look slippy, then,' said Mr Colclough.

'You can look as slippy as you like,' said Mr Brindley.

In another fifteen seconds we were in the car, and it had turned round, and was speeding towards Knype. A feverish journey! We passed electric cars every minute, and for three miles were continually twisting round the tails of ponderous, creaking, and excessively deliberate carts that dropped a trail of small coal, or huge barrels on wheels that dripped something like the finest Devonshire cream, or brewer's drays that left nothing behind them save a luscious odour of malt. It was a breathless slither over unctuous black mud through a long winding canon of brown-red houses and shops, with a glimpse here and there of a grey-green park, a canal, or a football field.

'I daredn't hurry,' said Mr Colclough, setting us down at the station. 'I was afraid of a skid.' He had not spoken during the transit.

'Don't put on side, Ol,' said Mr Brindley. 'What time did you get up this morning?'

'Eight o'clock, lad. I was at th' works at nine.'

He flew off to escape my thanks, and Mr Brindley and I went into the station. Owing to the celerity of the automobile we had half- an-hour to wait. We spent it chiefly at the bookstall. While we were there the extra-special edition of the STAFFORDSHIRE SIGNAL, affectionately termed 'the local rag' by its readers, arrived, and we watched a newsboy affix its poster to a board. The poster ran thus—

HANBRIDGE RATES LIVELY MEETING

—

KNYPE F.C. NEW CENTRE—FORWARD

—

ALL—WINNERS AND S.P.

Now, close by this poster was the poster of the DAILY TELEGRAPH, and among the items offered by the DAILY TELEGRAPH was: 'Death of Simon Fuge'. I could not forbear pointing out to Mr Brindley the difference between the two posters. A conversation ensued; and amid the rumbling of trains and the rough stir of the platform we got back again to Simon Fuge, and Mr Brindley's tone gradually grew, if not acrid, a little impatient.

'After all,' he said, 'rates are rates, especially in Hanbridge. And let me tell you that last season Knype Football Club jolly nearly got thrown out of the First League. The constitution of the team for this next season—why, damn it, it's a question of national importance! You don't understand these things. If Knype Football Club was put into the League Second Division, ten thousand homes would go into mourning. Who the devil was Simon Fuge?'

They joke with such extraordinary seriousness in the Five Towns that one is somehow bound to pretend that they are not joking. So I replied—

'He was a great artist. And this is his native district. Surely you ought to be proud of him!'

'He may have been a great artist,' said Mr Brindley, 'or he may not. But for us he was simply a man who came of a family that had a bad reputation for talking too much and acting the goat!'

'Well,' I said, We shall see—in fifty years.'

'That's just what we shan't,' said he. 'We shall be where Simon Fuge is—dead! However, perhaps we are proud of him. But you don't expect us to show it, do you? That's not our style.'

He performed the quasi-winking phenomenon with his eyes. It was his final exhibition of it to me.

'A strange place!' I reflected, as I ate my dinner in the dining- car, with the pressure of Mr Brindley's steely clasp still affecting my right hand, and the rich, honest cordiality of his au revoir in my heart. 'A place that is passing strange!'

And I thought further: He may have been a boaster, and a chatterer, and a man who suffered from cold feet at the wrong moments! And the Five Towns may have got the better of him, now. But that portrait of the little girl in the Wedgwood Institution is waiting there, right in the middle of the Five Towns. And one day the Five Towns will have to 'give it best'. They can say what they like! ... What eyes the fellow had, when he was in the right company!

IN A NEW BOTTLE

Commercial travellers are rather like bees; they take the seed of a good story from one district and deposit it in another.

Thus several localities, imperfectly righteous, have within recent years appropriated this story to their own annals. I once met an old herbalist from Wigan-Wigan of all places in beautiful England!—who positively asserted that the episode occurred just outside the London and North-Western main line station at Wigan. This old herbalist was no judge of the value of evidence. An undertaker from Hull told me flatly, little knowing who I was and where I came from, that he was the undertaker concerned in the episode. This undertaker was a liar. I use this term because there is no other word in the language which accurately expresses my meaning. Of persons who have taken the trouble to come over from the United States in order to inform me that the affair happened at Harper's Ferry, Poughkeepsie, Syracuse, Allegheny, Indianapolis, Columbus, Charlotte, Tabernacle, Alliance, Wheeling, Lynchburg, and Chicago it would be unbecoming to speak—they are best left to silence themselves by mutual recrimination. The fact is that the authentic scene of the affair was a third-class railway carriage belonging to the North Staffordshire Railway Company, and rolling on that company's loop-line between Longshaw and Hanbridge. The undertaker is now dead—it is a disturbing truth that even undertakers die sometimes—and since his widow has given me permission to mention his name, I shall mention his name. It was Edward Till. Of course everybody in the Five Towns knows who the undertaker was, and if anybody in the Five Towns should ever chance to come across this book, I offer him my excuses for having brought coals to Newcastle.

Mr Till used to be a fairly well-known figure in Hanbridge, which is the centre of undertaking, as it is of everything else, in the Five Towns. He was in a small but a successful way of business, had one leg a trifle shorter than the other (which slightly deteriorated the majesty of his demeanour on solemn occasions), played the fiddle, kept rabbits, and was of a forgetful disposition. It was possibly this forgetful disposition which had prevented him from rising into a large way of business. All admired his personal character and tempered geniality; but there are some things that will not bear forgetting. However, the story touches but lightly that side of his individuality.

One morning Mr Till had to go to Longshaw to fetch a baby's coffin which had been ordered under the mistaken impression that a certain baby was dead. This baby, I may mention, was the hero of the celebrated scare of Longshaw about the danger of being buried alive. The little thing had apparently passed away; and, what is more, an inquest had been held on it and its parents had been censured by the jury for criminal carelessness in overlaying it; and it was within five minutes of being nailed up, when it opened its eyes! You may imagine the enormous sensation that there was in the Five Towns. One doctor lost his reputation, naturally. He emigrated to the Continent, and now, practising at Lucerne in the summer and Mentone in the winter, charges fifteen shillings a visit (instead of three and six at Longshaw) for informing people who have nothing the matter with them that they must take care of themselves. The parents of the astonished baby moved the heaven and earth of the Five Towns to force the coroner to withdraw the stigma of the jury's censure; but they did not succeed, not even with the impassioned aid of two London halfpenny dailies.

To resume, Mr Till had to go to Longshaw. Now, unless you possess a most minute knowledge of your native country, you are probably not aware that in Aynsley Street, Longshaw, there is a provision dealer whose reputation for cheeses would be national and supreme if the whole of England thought as the Five Towns thinks.

'Teddy,' Mrs Till said, as Mr Till was starting, 'you might as well bring back with you a pound of Gorgonzola.' (Be it noted that I had the details of the conversation from the lady herself.)

'Yes,' said he enthusiastically, 'I will.'

'Don't go and forget it,' she enjoined him.

'No,' he said. 'I'll tie a knot in my handkerchief.'

'A lot of good that'll do!' she observed. 'You'd tied a knot in your handkerchief when you forgot that Councillor Barker's wife's funeral was altered from Tuesday to Monday.'

'Ah!' he replied. 'But now I've got a bad cold.'

'So you have!' she agreed, reassured.

He tied the knot in his handkerchief and went.

Thanks to his cold he did not pass the cheesemonger's without entering.

He adored Gorgonzola, and he reckoned that he knew a bit of good Gorgonzola when he met with it. Moreover, he and the cheesemonger were old friends, he having buried three of the cheesemonger's children. He emerged from the cheesemonger's with a pound of the perfectest Gorgonzola that ever greeted the senses.

The abode of the censured parents was close by, and also close to the station. He obtained the coffin without parley, and told the mother, who showed him the remarkable child with pride, that under the circumstances he should make no charge at all. It was a ridiculously small coffin. He was quite accustomed to coffins. Hence he did the natural thing. He tucked the little coffin under one arm, and, dangling the cheese (neat in brown paper and string) from the other hand, he hastened to the station. With his unmatched legs he must have made a somewhat noticeable figure.

A loop-line train was waiting, and he got into it, put the cheese on the rack in a corner, and the coffin next to it, assured himself that he had not mislaid his return ticket, and sat down under his baggage. It was the slackest time of day, and, as the train started at Longshaw, there were very few passengers. He had the compartment to himself.

He was just giving way to one of those moods of vague and pleasant meditation which are perhaps the chief joy of such a temperament, when he suddenly sprang up as if in fear. And fear had in fact seized him. Suppose he forgot those belongings on the rack? Suppose, sublimely careless, he descended from the train and left them there? What a calamity! And similar misadventures had happened to him before. It was the cheese that disquieted him. No one would be sufficiently unprincipled to steal the coffin, and he would ultimately recover it at the lost luggage office, babies' coffins not abounding on the North Staffordshire Railway. But the cheese! He would never see the cheese again! No integrity would be able to withstand the blandishments of that cheese. Moreover, his wife would be saddened. And for her he had a sincere and profound affection.

His act of precaution was to lift the coffin down from the rack, and place it on the seat beside him, and then to put the parcel of cheese on the coffin. He surveyed the cheese on the coffin; he surveyed it with the critical and experienced eye of an undertaker, and he decided that, if anyone else got into the carriage, it would not look quite decent, quite becoming—in a word, quite nice. A coffin is a coffin, and people's feelings have to be considered.

So he whipped off the lid of the coffin, stuck the cheese inside, and popped the lid on again. And he kept his hand on the coffin that he might not forget it. When the train halted at Knype, Mr Till was glad that he had put the cheese inside, for another passenger got into the compartment. And it was a clergyman. He recognized the clergyman, though the clergyman did not recognize him. It was the Reverend Claud ffolliott, famous throughout the Five Towns as the man who begins his name with a small letter, doesn't smoke, of course doesn't drink, but goes to football matches, has an average of eighteen at cricket, and makes a very pretty show with the gloves, in spite of his thirty-eight years; celibate, very High, very natty and learned about vestments, terrific at sick couches and funerals. Mr Till inwardly trembled to think what the Reverend Claud ffolliott might have said had he seen the cheese reposing in the coffin, though the coffin was empty.

The parson, whose mind was apparently occupied, dropped into the nearest corner, which chanced to be the corner farthest away from Mr Till. He then instantly opened a copy of The Church Times and began to read it, and the train went forward. The parson sniffed, absently, as if he had been dozing and a fly had tickled his nose. Shortly afterwards he sniffed again, but without looking up from his perusals. He sniffed a third time, and glanced over the top edge of THE CHURCH TIMES at Mr Till. Calmed by the innocuous aspect of Mr Till, he bent once more to the paper. But after an interval he was sniffing furiously. He glanced at the window; it was open. Finally he lowered The CHURCH TIMES, as who should say: 'I am a long-suffering man, but really this phenomenon which assaults my nostrils must be seriously inquired into.'

Then it was that he caught sight of the coffin, with Mr Till's hand caressing it, and Mr Till all in black and carrying a funereal expression. He straightened himself, pulled himself together on account of his cloth, and said to Mr Till in his most majestic and sympathetic graveside voice—

'Ah! my dear friend, I see that you have suffered a sad, sad bereavement.'

That rich, resonant voice was positively thrilling when it addressed hopeless grief. Mr Till did not know what to say, nor where to look.

'You have, however, one thing to be thankful for, very thankful for,' said the parson after a pause, 'you may be sure the poor thing is not in a trance.'

Also Published by the Echo Library By Arnold Bennett

NOVELS
Leonora
Sacred and Profane Love
Buried Alive
The Old Wives' Tale
Helen with the High Hand
Hilda Lessways
The Card
The Regent
The Price of Love
The Lion's Share
The Pretty Lady

FANTASIAS

The Grand Babylon Hotel

SHORT STORIES

Tales of the Five Towns
The Grim Smile of the Five Towns
The Matador of the Five Towns

BELLES-LETTRES

Over There
The Author's Craft (In Large Print)

Printed in the United Kingdom
by Lightning Source UK Ltd.
110296UKS00001B/211

9 781846 376627